Love & Urban Melodrama

High time you started thinking.

Love & Urban Melodrama

High time you started thinking.

Shantanu Anam

Srishti
PUBLISHERS & DISTRIBUTORS

Srishti Publishers & Distributors
N-16, C. R. Park
New Delhi 110 019
srishtipublishers@gmail.com

First published by Srishti Publishers & Distributors in 2011

Typeset in AGaramond 11pt. by Suresh Kumar Sharma at Srishti

Printed and bound in India

The Author's Note

The ability of Indians to worship nearly everything freaks me out just a bit.

I mean to say that I love music, but how does that justify having a music goddess, or an education goddess, we worship the Cow for god's sake.

Not that I intend to offend anyone, but its not just the Hindus whose animal worship makes us see the surplus livestock roam aimlessly around our state of the art grade separators and no one really giving a fuck.

Education is something that ensures a secure feeling within a person till he moves to the next world(Which in my opinion comprises of other burnt ash flowing around before one joins a filth infested water source).

I was having a rather intense conversation with a rather dear friend named Anusha the other day, and just as I felt that I was entirely in a agreement with her on her take on the education system, I realized quite a few things.

1. She was my first girlfriend.
2. The first point could be ignored, so what I was saying was that she was expressing her take on professional courses and the toll they take on students trying to achieve something out of them.
3. There will always be people who would manage to derive what exactly is supposed to be extracted out of these, which is nothing virtually, but a neat looking package.

4. But when I talk about feeling secure, I hardly mean it financially, its NOT about knowing something more than what others know, or perhaps earning more than how much others earn(I wouldn't complain though).
5. It's about being able to encounter the same thing as thing as others in the world and yet managing to view it with ones own perspective, if everyone was to feel the same way on observing something, the 'mind' of an individual would probably genetically mutate to resemble a genital organ, that would get excited from time to time, have nothing much to say though!!!
6. I am certainly not an authority to make a comment on the education system(Only If others writing could understand this, and stop maintaining double standards for once), so I wont say much except; Velleity that loosely translates to 'free will'.
7. For those of you who have an option to exercise the above written word, do it by all means.

Siddharth: College

True story, well the need to make this confession is based on the fact that there is a significant similarity in the way in which both our college lives unfolded.

The need for our parents to educate us 'well' is understandable, and is a practice that we would religiously follow up with our off springs as well.

I somehow feel that what the widening generation gap is altering is the very concept of education.

Its something that has been perceived in a similar way by a majority of the people except the one odd idiots who are spoken about in shushed voices by the pan chewing uncle-jee and the saree-saunth clad aunty-jee's.

I am certainly not trying to put down the very concept of formal education but does a piece of paper with a couple of marks thrown in really define a person for what he is or manage to gauge what is the likely contribution he is going to make to the society.

If your answer is yes, well best of luck but remember no matter how hard you work to make the 'piece of paper' look good, you are going to stop questioning yourself as to why the paper came about in the first place. And the day we stop questioning things around is the way we stop growing as people.

Demarcations need to be made in terms of the people who are capable of handling jobs that are easy and those that aren't .

But is a maze of classrooms, lectures and boring yet rigorous assignments the right method to be adopted to make these demarcations.

My answer is a flat no based on series of reasons, I will start with a few of them.

1. Individuality is a word that something that a lot of people stress on when they seek professionals for selling soaps and toothpastes.
2. The aim is not to put down market oriented strategies, well I use toothpaste every now and then which in turn causes my need to buy it which explains the need for these firms to strategize their sales.

3. How can Individuality be sought when the prerequisite to getting an opportunity to showcase it is possessing the same degree as a thousand others who are, well, also trying to establish themselves and their uniqueness.
4. This task is obviously an uphill one considering there is NO difference between the thousands and lakhs of people who leave home in their sleek sedans to place themselves in thee comfort of their claustrophobic cubicles.

Siddharth Speaks

Long back, I remember encountering a piece somewhere that spoke of the four stages which a person went through in life, one which involved knowledge, another sexuality, spirituality and so on.

If there was one phase in modern day times that helped in the process of these three occurring simultaneously, it's the stoner phase.

Reality Shows:

1. Gay shit.
2. Gay shit(To emphasize)
3. Unnecessary melodrama.
4. Won't waste more time on them.

Foreword

So here it goes, I have no clue as to why I did this, why I felt the need to ensure I make a record of my present mental state. Perhaps I'm sub-consciously aware of some of the grotesque murders I'm likely to commit and thus decided to have a recorded proof of my senility. My parents were extremely helpful in this pursuit of mine, they asked me to turn off the music every night, and there are so many things one does in an environment of pin drop silence, when one is wide awake in the middle of the night.

There are a lot of people who I intend to thank for being extremely helpful and want to thank even those who did not grace me with their ridiculous presence.

Srishti Publishers for taking this risk and being so amazingly professional and helpful, it is just awesome.

Mr Rakesh Duda a.k.a. Babla Mama for just being there.

"The Pretty Poet", for making the feeling of hatred and being thirty seem all right once in a while, and my sister Rishika for treating me like a kid brother, hope she continues to do so for a while. I started blogging a while back, and the informal approach probably extends to my writing style, so forgive me keeping in mind that I'm only a silly teenager.

Special Thank you's to Abhishek Marwaha for being there, Rahul Bhatnagar for impressing with his short stint and Shweta Vishwanthan and Annesha Sil for being awesome.

Shweta, you know what's next.

Ayan Mukherjee, for being there, in trying times and situations, and this is true for Varun 'Shiv' Nanda, Akshay 'Yash' Dewan, Shivani Gupta, Ranbeer, Ishan, Sanjay and others who won't forgive me perhaps.

Meet the Characters:

SIDDHARTH

My hero!! The reasons I have for using this particular name are plentiful. I remember when I was young and innocent(relatively speaking,don't smirk), my parents convinced me of the fact that I had an elder brother who was away at boarding school. The point of this fictional offspring of theirs was to get work done.(I have discussed this extensively on my blog, check the URL on the back).

Siddharth has a lot of attributes that I admire , for instance his ability to lose focus instantly and also how he never managed to realize how humour has never,will never take anyone anywhere. But to his credit, the poor guy doesn't want to go anywhere. Keeping in mind the rather simplistic plot and rather scarcely talented author, the characterization might not be very intrinsic but I certainly feel that there is a connection that Sid forms at least.

There are so many things about Sid that you wouldn't know considering that Sid is certainly not a figment of my imagination who I cooked up and tried to make seem believable because I was bored.

Siddharth is the person I have related to the most in a long time, you know how one tends to compare attributes of people surrounding you to yours and eventually realize that there are the one odd people who react to situations and people in a similar way to you and thus you want to extend your association with them, that, to put it simply is why I am writing.

Kavi:

She is the only other character who needs an introduction in this segment.

Kavi being the girl with a mind of her own tucked away consciously to attract too much attention and beautifully packaged with good looks buzzing vaguely with bad songs makes the most loveable person in the book.

At the outset, all I could say about her is the following;

1. She is emotionally unstable, yet happy.
2. Was, is and would continue to be Sid's best friend, till they're thirty though, that's when the wedding bells arrive.
3. An integral part of what awaits you as you turn the page.
4. The cutest hippie around.

1

BIRTHDAY WISHES AND FLASHING

The silence in the room was amazing .
15th September
2006
08:07 a.m.
Bedroom

I would have been up at least an hour back, if it was a regular day. It's probably Sunday, I thought to myself. I checked my watch, the 15th of September, Sunday it was. Fifteenth I wondered, there was something that I was trying to remember desperately about this day. The mid semester exam results were to come out, no, it was something else. Those I was flunking anyway. "Holy Fuck" , I screamed and lunged for my phone. "Hello Neeta, hello, hello," how could I forget Neeta's birthday. After another eighty odd calls which were cut mercilessly, I decided to get some breakfast. "Good morning son", mom said half mockingly, she was probably witnessing my futile attempts to get through to Neeta, he thought. "So, big day huh, what plans", she was just making things worse. He focused on his French toast with new found vengeance. "I wished her at night you know." Fuck the French toast he thought. "Why wouldn't you remind me ma, why, what pleasure do you get in doing this." That accusation was unfairly made as if this had been a regular deal with my mom. "I thought you would have already wished her Sid, how was I to know that you haven't", she said with the same innocence with which she had said "you look tired, why don't you crash early,' the previous night. "Achha sorry, take money, go get her a gift, something nice". Something nice, said with a glazed look in my mom's eyes expecting me to hear that, and promptly buy a big teddy bear perhaps and stand outside Neeta's place only to get it flung back at me. "Mom, I've already bought her a dress, just talk to her and find out if she's at home won't you. I'm going for a shower, there's that new Gerard Butler movie that released this week, we'll go for that, then there's class at six. "I'd met Neeta about a year back at these tuitions I was taking to help me get through my final episode of schooling where I was battling Physics and Chemistry and losing miserably. There are those who sing in showers, then there are those who dance, and those who well, do other dirty things. I'm the freak who does nothing and is motionless waiting for the shampoo to come off. Just hope she cools off by the time I reach her place.

Trrring
Neeta's doorbell
11:00 a.m.
"Hello aunty, good morning, is Neeta home." This confidence seemed to vaporize every time I encountered Brig Mukherjee though. "Mounindrmegoodhello", my regular greeting was blurted on sighting his large frame and he grunted while making a drink. "Should I make you a drink beta", my suspicion was that he was waiting for the day I'd say yes and he tie me up and make me his bitch for good. I refused politely while imagining myself stark naked with the Brigadier pitching with the scotch in his hand.

"Ahem, sniff," Neeta came out looking drop dead gorgeous. Ok, Neeta is a looker, a major looker, I on the other hand have been mistaken for a salesman from time to time while out shopping. "Where are you kids heading", I was naked again.

Thankfully Neeta handled the talking when it came to her father. My mom had already broken the news of the movie plan to her over the phone, so much for surprising her.

"Is that what you are going to wear," Neeta asked icily when we were looking for an auto to get to Saket. "No, I plan to go home, change into something that you would not like anyway and come back while I keep you waiting like a fool in the auto when I've already goofed up enough to make the person who is most special to me in the whole world, sad on her birthday." Home run, I forgot to mention, she was the looker, I was the talker. After a long session of hugging and kissing in the auto and after a very awkward minute of eye contact with smirking horny autorickshaw driver, we reached Saket.

Saket is the hub for all kids who bunk school and for those who have nothing much to do in life, second to Priya market though. It was taboo to consider going there, especially with Neeta. "So, you're a major now huh", I said with an evil smirk, as we paid the auto guy who obviously was checking out Neeta and I couldn't really blame him.

"Avniiiiiii", she screamed and ran towards the anorexic bitch. Avni was a friend of hers who we bumped into more often than necessary. Oh and yeah, she hated me. "You can do so much better", was like a chant that she'd have for Neeta the moment I was out of sight.

"Hi Avni", I said as if my balls were clasped by a crab. She reciprocated with a "looking good ya Sid, lost some weight have you." The nudging continued and I kept mum till she left, I knew where she was going, probably getting sloshed in some cheap ass bar and hooking up with guys she wouldn't even remember the next day. It amazed me how these two were such good friends.

"Gerard Butler is so hot, it's not even funny," Neeta said earnestly as if she'd seen every frame of the movie. I liked the movie though, I liked every movie, whatever little I saw of it anyway. It was about how a guy dies and leaves letters so as help his wife to move on. Kind of gay but I liked it nonetheless. "We have class at six, what class do we have again."I think we had Organic Chemistry, random Egyptian hieroglyphs made more sense to me than those stupid dots and hyphens jutting out of carbon atoms, Neeta was marginally better at academics, more importantly she tried. "Chemistry." Silence, the rest of the movie got more morbid and gay so we decided to stop watching, I would have stopped watching either way, but Gerard Butler didn't figure much in the second half so the decision was mutual.

I had to get back home and go through a script for an interschool we had in a week. The dramatics society was all that managed to drag me to school in the morning and the practice slips provided valid reasons for me to escape from classes that I'd end up sleeping through anyway.

"Siddharth , Siddharth." I'd fallen asleep in tuitions again, I knew he was going to throw a fit. Five days in a row, anyone would. "Don't Enter Thees Kilaas Again," he spat and I left.

10:00 p.m.
Bedroom
"You got thrown out of class Siddharth," it's amazing how Sid no longer existed once the temper rose. "Yes ma, I was tired so I ended up sleeping".

"I just have one question for you Sid, how do you plan on passing the school finals." This question I asked myself everyday too, but I knew I'd manage, I just needed a month and I'd be sorted, hopefully. "Mom, don't worry, I will manage, the movie is very good".

Tring Tring. "Oyee Varun, where the fuck have you been man. Cool then, let's meet tomorrow at three."

Varun had been like a brother all along until he started dating that maniac who hogged all his time. He was an ideal student, had a killer sense of humour and would always be there for friends when he was needed. He was dating this freak who was somehow under the impression that it was important for Varun to either be with her or on the phone with her. She killed his social life. His grades dropped, and the sad part was that he really liked her.

Neeta seemed more and more angelic to me the more I thought of these clingy possessive girls.

I was considered a good actor. I mean I was good enough to call the shots on casting and was consulted about adjustments in the scripts and character profiles.

"Wake up!!" my mom said as she splashed water, wonder why she couldn't do only one of the two. I slipped into uniform and left.

Today was the day we had the competition, in Neeta's school. The absence of god got reiterated by the fact that I had to pick a role where I was required to wear harem pants for this competition in particular.

Neeta studied in this brat school where the guys were brats. Sorry but that's the only description that fits, it's impossible to elaborate, the girls though were hot, my Neeta being a shining example.

About the harem pants, the problem kind of started when I wore pants that were a size larger. Oh and I forgot, what are they called, underclothes.

The cue for Aman to get down on my feet was 'thou not makest thou my wife' or something like that.

So this is what exactly happened, "thou not makest thou my wife", my voice boomed in the auditorium. Aman tripped, the bastard, and yanked my pants around my knees to support himself. Well he didn't fall, my pants did though. Now I was naked in front of Neeta's entire school, I didn't have too many options. This is how I went about it.

"Thouest wanting mou body."

I still hadn't pulled them up.

Advise, the easiest thing to do is bullshit Shakespearean English.

"Thouest wantest my body, yest yonder not wanting mou heart."

I still hadn't pulled them up.

"Mouest man of love, thouest woman of body, yonder ponder et tu amania."

Still down my pants were, Aman bordering on breaking into a laugh caught on to what I was trying and came up with a brilliant "mouest wantest thouest heart, not body" and pulled my pants up and hugged me.

We came first, and I flashed the cockiest school in town.

16th September
03:00 p.m.
Bedroom

I was still reeling under the impact of the competition and Neeta's expression when I met her later. Was refusing to believe that I had intentionally not pulled my pants up in front of nearly a thousand kids. I managed to sleep though it was disturbed considering the fact that I kept seeing naked me in the auditorium and Neeta's dad eyeing me lecherously with a drink in his hand. Sid, the only hope you have of being at peace with yourself is accepting a drink , I thought to myself. Big deal, what's the worst that could happen, a hangover, a sore behind. No, never happening, better sense prevailed at last.

The bell rang, Varun I figured. He looked pathetic, the groomed stud who never spent less than an hour in front of the mirror was a mess. "Dude, what the fuck is up with you man. Have you looked at yourself? Facial hair is a no-no remember, unless you're forty or those paharganj freaks who roam around clueless of their surroundings. You smell of alcohol, you're a fucking mess man."I told him to sit and went to look for food in the fridge, "Varun, leftover chicken, cool," he nodded and headed towards the verandah.

He lit a smoke and spoke, "Sid, I flunked every fucking exam man. My parents haven't spoken to me for a week. I was grounded for like two weeks and was'nt allowed phone calls. As if that's not enough Shikha started dating someone else, she says that if I don't have time for her, she might as well find someone who cares more. I haven't spoken to her man, she refuses to answer my calls or respond to my messages. She's blocked me on msn and the works bro, anyway I guess I'm fine".

I continued to stare at him in disbelief, "All that we will handle, why the fuck are you smoking man".

"Trust me Sid, it helps", he said as he took a dangerously long drag of the cancer stick in his hand.

"Helps Varun, helps what Varun, helps in the process of achieving an early and untimely death perhaps, aur kaise," I said that and disappeared to get a deo back from my room, all I needed now was my mother to smell smoke at home.

If he had failed every paper, my chances seemed rather bleak, but that I'd worry about later. It was Operation Varun right now.

"Oyee Varun , listen, how long were you dating this Shikha, about a year right? Now I clearly remember two major fights that you spoke to me about in this supposedly blissful year for you. Dude, she was a bitch and you know it man. She never paid at dates, never let you spend time with people you liked, she never let you spend time with people you knew before her, Varun she never let you spend time with me man. I've known you for eleven fucking years and you virtually gave up on talking to me for the past one year man. I knew this had to happen sooner or later and I'm sorry if this hurts you, but I'm really happy this happened. And honestly speaking, she was kind of bluh bluh, bastard you know what I mean. Listen bro, in the words of the greatest nameless philosopher of our times man, "Fuck the shit bro." Now toss that smoke aur chal, lets go inside."

Maybe I was convincing, maybe I wasn't but he sure was listening to every word of mine in rapt attention.

Varun and I had been classmates forever and if it wasn't for his notes and chits, my tenure as his classmate would have ended long back.

"Listen Varun, first of all shave and wash up, I have a plan." I handed him a disposable razor that I'd seen lying around strangely for a long time next to my monitor. He went inside and came out looking cleaner, more like the Varun I knew.

"We need to pass, it's essential if we want to make anything of our lives. And we also know that we are the laziest bastards on the face of this earth who wouldn't put in a minute more than required to prepare for this exam which made others around us crap in their pants periodically. Let's start studying together man, we'll start early and maybe we can pass with respectable marks. Neeta can join us from time to time and her notes are the shit man, she colour codes them and the works. Never really understood why she barely manages to pass after all the effort. Then again god endowed her with a face and curves that would remain the same irrespective of her marks and most importantly, that smile..."Varun snapped, " Listen lover boye, you can fantasize about your girlfriend when you're alone. You don't need to put me through this considering how I'll be back to having imaginary conversations with Shyla Stylez and Jenna Jameson, if I continue to stay single for too long". These two are, well! professionals who work in the field of performing arts, yeah lets keep it at that.

"I like the study together scene you're talking about but when do we start".

215 (Two hundred and fifteen days later)
18th April
02:12 a.m.

"Sid , Physics board exam day after man. We have eight chapters left, fuck you man."Varun's panic attacks were pissing the daylights out of me. "Listen Varun, don't be a wuss. There is no need to panic, remember we read all the chapters a month back, now isn't the time to study, it's the time to gather ourselves."Such a wuss he was, we had read every line in the physics textbook once, what else one could possibly do.

"Sid, they don't ask questions about the text, it's all about derivations and numericals and the works, please let's study".

"Ok Varun, the most that I'll do is learn the solutions to the previous two years papers, not a word more", and I'd got myself a deal. We mugged the Greek symbols which my teacher drew in class everyday while we were too busy playing twenty questions and tic-tac-toe. The charm associated with the game vanishes outside the four walls of a classroom. If one was to approach a girl in a bar and draw parallel bars on a tissue paper, he'd almost get slapped, same guy would get a sheepish inviting grin as if to say 'you win this one and I'll sleep with you,' if he asked in a classroom.

2

THE RESULT AND THE SLAP(s) ROMANTIC FLASHBACK HASH AND VELLORE

10th May
01:10 a.m.
Bedroom

I sat staring at the walls. The results were expected in a couple of hours. The official time was six in the morning but the results were uploaded a couple of hours earlier usually. Mom was pretending to be asleep but I was dead sure she was awake and saying her silent prayers to make her hopeless idiot of a son a school passout. I had never figured passing out of school would have been such a headache .Cousin's doing MBAs , others research scholar at Ivy leagues, here I was praying that I'd have a school leaving certificate in hand. Nicotine had made a silent and forceful entry into my life for about a month (Neeta sulked, it definitely helped).The stress levels had risen as I knew that even if I managed to pass the exams, getting into college would be a major headache as it was futile to apply in Delhi University with cut-offs skyrocketing every year.

"Mom, it's out," I screamed as I fed my name and registration number.

Siddharth Kumar	
English	47
Physics	65
Chemistry	53
Maths	54
Economics	59
Result	PASS

I stared at it blankly for a minute .No wait, I definitely stared longer because when I stopped staring my elated mother was making phone calls to everyone she could to let them know that her son had passed out of school contrary to what she and a lot of other people were expecting. Then started two levels of conversation which were equally annoyeing. "You were always a smart kid, never really needed to study did you, a little more effort and you might have topped."

I hadn't spoken since. I was staring at the English and Economics score. I knew for a fact that my English was relatively much better than those I knew and was a bit shocked to later learn that I had scored the least in my school in that subject.

Varun had done better, he'd scored a consistent ten odd marks more than me in every subject except English, where he managed a ninety. A fucking ninety I thought as I went out for a smoke to the nearby pan shop. He had consulted me on all doubts he had with the literature and I corrected his grammatical errors on a regular basis, either I was an awesome teacher or the examiners had screwed me over. “Bhaiya, two milds, one thums up”, I said and sat down trying to figure out what I would do. It was impossible for me to apply in any arts college with a sub-fifty score in English .I would be rejected immediately. I decided to call up Neeta, she had managed a smooth sixty and was rather happy when I had called earlier.

“Hello, Good morning uncle. Yes, definitely, I will be there. He'd asked me to come over.

10th May
Trrring
Neeta's place
11:00 a.m.

“Hi Sid, sit down, we wanted to talk to you,” her mother said as I entered. We, what could she mean by we, probably she and Neeta. But I knew this we was different , I just had a very strange feeling that I wasn't going to like what 'we' were going to say to me.

“Sid, we saw your result. We thought we needed to talk to you after the result.” Neeta entered silently and sat in the corner, she was staring at the floor motionless.

“Sid, no college is going to accept you with marks like that. And out of all the entrances you attempted, the only one where you figured in the list is that Vellore college where you quite certainly won't go because you are very creative, the most talented person on the face of this earth.”The sarcastic bastard was making a second and he certainly had more to say.

"Sid, all this drama, debate is nothing, your mother probably encourages you because she doesn't know better. I'm sure if your dad hadn't walked out on you guys, he would have told you how these are immaterial in the long run."

Silence. Ouch. Time to speak Sid.

"Make me a drink, on the rocks. My dad, my issue, I've handled my life pretty well without him and my Mom never really let me feel his absence in any way. And about my getting into a college, I assure you that will happen." I gulped down my drink and continued speaking.

" I still can't believe the pointlessness of your calling me here. And after doing so, what gives you the right to discuss my father. Now that you've raised the issue, I'll tell you one thing, not having a dad around is better than one who starts drinking at eight in the morning and drools on the carpet like a fool".

Thud.

Thish.

Those were two very hard slaps deposited on my face by Neeta.

"Listen, my dad had called you here to ask you whether you required any help to get into a college. He knows a few people back home and he wanted you to go to a decent college. You major fuck up, how you dare talk to my dad like that"

Thish. One more. She didn't look so pretty.

"Get the fuck out of this house and don't call, ever. I'm breaking up with you because you, Sid are a retard and a worthless piece of shit. I regret every second of my life I have wasted around you".

There is so much that happens in one's life that it's impossible to sit down and be upset about something. Neeta, was the coolest person I knew and the best friend I had. It had been a week and she refused to answer my calls or respond to my messages. I was getting the Varun treatment. She, though, had taken it a step further and called up my Mother and told her to get the point across to me that I will never be able to talk to her again.

Sid And Neeta: The Flashback

Well, the two years of being in a relationship had helped gather a lot of memories, good and bad. Play the mushy songs you associate with love stories, I'm delving into mine.

Neeta Mukherjee to me is the epitome of beauty, the nicest girl I have ever met. The fact that our relationship had lasted this long spoke volumes about either how special 'We' were or how her optic nerve was paying the fool with her blind spot.

Anyway, the reason as to why I am feeling that I need to discuss how Neeta and I spend our time together is because one learns from stupidity only if he never forgets it and ensures it haunts him for some time at least.

Café Coffee Gay

Ask any red blooded committed guy how many times he has felt that what he has, is and will continue to be doing is rather irritating and idiotically mushy at times.

'Café Coffee Gay' is a story of pain, betrayal, lust and power.

Wait, no it's not, it's just about how I sang a really gay song in the coffee shop for Neeta.

Now before you start to get all judgemental, this is what really happened.

Home
10 A.M.

"Mom, before you leave for work, leave some money, meeting Neeta today".

I was tired from the previous nights phone conversation, which eventually ended up terminating only when the sixty year olds were through with their yoga and had probably left for their ridiculously early morning walks.

For god's sake, leave when there are people around, what if you get mugged, the little stick to shoo away stray pups is the only armament you have anyway.

I brushed my teeth and moved towards the flower pot that had my smokes, I needed one to get my well, system moving.

Neeta had been attending classes to prepare for Architecture, I had been meeting Neeta, and Varun, and also this funny bastard down from school, who incidentally shared a post with me in the school council.

Yuvraj, incidentally, for a name which oozed talent and outright crass retro sexuality, he was an idiot.

Varun needed help with some decision he had take on joining a college nearby, well he was quite certain he would join his dad's business in a couple of years so he needed a degree that would probably get him a 'fair, convent educated girl' through those shady matrimonial services in a couple of years.

At least he had a plan, I was still clueless about what I was to do in life.

I could go on ridiculing those who had compromised in terms of picking out the courses they would like to pursue or those who had chosen smart course in non descript institutions, but I knew at they had a plan of sorts.

When it came to Aunties asking me what I intended to do, I muttered a casual 'MBA', I mean I knew that was one answer which wouldn't be skeptically viewed, they even forgot to ask what graduation I intended to pursue once their ears were soothed by the the three letters that made everyone, from middle aged men to young skimpily clad women do a back flip.

So this I how the day unfolded.

"Hey, Sid, what's with your maid, she totally checks me out man, how messed up is that."

I felt for some very strange reason that his ego was getting just the slightest boost caused by my supposedly lecherous maid.

I never felt she was, or maybe she just subjected Varun to her 'watchful gaze'.

She freaked me out nonetheless, and come to think of it didn't exactly do much work around the house.

Any way, getting back to the CCG day, its amazing how Indian I am.

What I mean is how many Indian are capable of transforming any rational sane conversation into one that involves bitching about domestic help?

I'd say each and every one of them, even the domestic help have the same network where they bitch about their respective employeers.

Getting back to where we were, I told Varun that we could go out for coffee and Neeta could meet us there, and we could figure out what exactly he should be doing.

CCG
Café Coffee Gay
1 PM
"One doppio, and a café Frappe", this is probably a sentence I had said the most in my life."

Varun had walked out for a bit and intended to be back in a while, call from some girl he was semi-dating or something, it sounded pretty much like benefits when he described the relationship profile.

Neeta and I had grown accustomed to the concept of PDA and our make out sessions were rather inappropriate and were just generally awkward except for those few lucky occasions where we were at home.

She asked me what I was doing in a while, and considering how busy I had been of late, I checked up with my non existent daily planner to realize if I was free to go over to her place afterwards.

"Check this out, its semi-acoustic", Varun walked in with a guitar and started strumming out of the blue, he started paying Hey There Delilah and I stupidly enough was convinced to sing along by my girlfriend who didn't really give a fuck about me possibly feeling just a tad awkward due to the presence of others there.

Later:

Neeta's Place:

I kissed her slowly and I held her hand up against the wall.

She looked really pretty, I picked her up and took her to the room.

After an eternity, her top finally came off, I undid her hair and kissed her a bit more.

There was hardly anything that I could say.

" You do know, we could talk also", she said as she took the hook off her bra, I mean who combines an action like that with the sentence she unleashed.

My mind threw an immediate 'No, not now we can't!!'.

She took off my shirt and positioned herself on top, then she started kissing me back so hard that I could swear my lips had a gash.

That's pretty much all my memory holds in store for you, and for me(unfortunately).

17th May
Basant Lok
06:00 p.m.

I was standing outside the this smoke's shop right across Modern Bazaar where I'd always bump into an uncle or an aunty who'd give me a dirty look on seeing me with a smoke and ask me if my mother knew about it. I was waiting for Varun , we planned to go catch a movie.

"Oyee, tickets are sold out freak, what do we do now."

"Drink," pat came my reply.

'Hash' is this place known for its cheap alcohol and the fact that it's always dark for those couples who need to, well, pray.

Varun and I were three large rum and cokes down when I started speaking.

"Bhai, listen to me. I have no family business to rely on like you, it's time I started to figure out what I want to do man. Because now I have absolutely no time and no options also man. I'm screwed majorly. Neeta was right, I am a major fuck up. I need to start figuring out what my options are, oyee! repeat yaar."I called for another drink keeping in mind the fact that Mom was away at my grandparents place and I could go home sloshed.

"Varun, there's some college in Vellore which I miraculously cleared the entrance for Vellore Engineering College, but Varun, how am I supposed to manage a course like that bro".

I kept silent and worked my way through my pack of milds.

"Sid, it's not important what degree you have man. One doesn't necessarily have to fix machines once he's an engineer man. Just go, give it a shot. Get the degree and come back man. You can do something more like you in your post graduation, its not like there are plenty of options available anyway."

Physics, sixty five. That after browsing through the chapters once. Maybe I did have an aptitude for doing this, and even if I didn't , it's not like I was rejecting college offers everyday.

I couldn't sleep a minute that night. I kept thinking about what I could do except for going to VEC. I certainly couldn't hang around in Delhi any longer without getting into a college. Everyone I knew was into college by now, even Varun had gone and gotten himself into a business administration programme in some private university in the outskirts of Delhi.

Vellore then, I thought as I finally fell asleep.

To: Neeta Mukherjee

Subject: Bye

Hi, long time right. I'm sorry for my behaviour that day. I'm going away to college next week. It's an engineering college called VEC. It's somewhere in Tamil Nadu. Can you imagine me doing engineering, but I guess I'll have to. I tried calling you a number of times. You must have been busy. I messaged you also, no reply. Maybe you don't want to talk to me anymore, that's just fine. I've spoken to them, I just have to carry my certificates and the demand drafts because I missed the counseling and I'm being admitted on extra payment into whichever branch. I always thought engineering was engineering, no branches. Remember the time we were talking to that engineer who was a trainee at PVR when we went for that Aamir movie. It's not funny how you dragged me for it, you couldn't get your eyes off the screen for a second. I couldn't get mine off you.

There are times when I feel sad Neeta, very sad. Not because we broke up, I knew you could do a lot better. Probably because of the fact that I lost my best friend too in the process. You know how I've spoken to you about everything under the sun for the past two years. Who do I go to now Neeta ? I'm sure you are very happy now that I'm not there to piss you off with my lame corny jokes.

I miss you a lot. I love you. Could you do me a favour? Meet me once. I really feel the need to meet once more before I leave for college.

There are plenty of better guys out there for you Neeta, I don't want you back.

It's just that I want to meet. We both know how awesome the two years were and this is not how they needed to end.

All I want is to meet to say bye, I'm sorry if that's asking for too much.

Take care

I love you

Bye

She replied.

Dear Sid,

Don't mail me ever again.

Fuck off

Ok, not exactly what I had expected. There's nothing one could do about it anyway.

She had decided to play the role of a cold hearted bitch to perfection and it came so naturally to her. I was amazed. Now I saw where she connected with that Avni. Avni I figured must have contributed significantly to this situation the moment she must have seen an opening. Now of course she had a handful of reasons to throw at Neeta, no career, no manners, no looks, no six pack.......No Neeta , I hadn't imagined ties with someone like Neeta could get this severed. She was still talking to all my friends normally but refused to discuss me with any of them. I was pathetic enough to get my friends into talking to her to figure out why she was doing this.

"All packed", my Mom asked as I stuffed more socks into my suitcase.

Considering their negligent size and monetary value, the priority given by people to these while packing always is amazing. Fuck the wallet, have you put in your socks.

The best part was that I was leaving for a college where none of my friends or friend's friends or friend's friend's friends were going. This was going to be some experience that I was about embarking on.

Four years was a long time but then again it seemed like yesterday that I was in the ninth grade so hopefully I will be back here smiling about how I managed an engineering degree somehow four years from now.

I had checked the details of the college online. The hostels and the food seemed really good. Also, they had clubs like theatre and debating, so I wasn't very wary of the place. From the pictures uploaded on the website, the crowd seemed rather cosmopolitan for its location. Vellore is located at a distance of about a hundred kilometers from Chennai, the capital of Tamil Nadu.

What I was happy about was that Bangalore was just three hours away in case I needed a break ever. The most fucked up part was that due to my skipping the normal admission procedure, I was ending up paying nearly five times what others were and to top it off was stuck in a branch that only those who had supernormal intelligence or an ability to churn your ass off sixteen hours a day chose.

Electronics and Telematics, no telecommunication, no it was just communication I feel,'ban gaya tu engineer' I thought to myself and went to take a good look at my room before I left.

I had tried calling Neeta again, it was kind of fucked considering how I was confident. she wouldn't pick up no matter how many times I tried. Well at least she didn't disappoint there.

"Bye Mom, the cab's here. I'll call from the Chennai airport. Don't worry Mom, I'll manage."

My mother was happy about the fact that I had gotten into college but couldn't understand as to why I needed to pick a course this tough.

Though she knew it was sheer lack of options which made me do this. Varun was coming to the airport to drop me off. I had to pick him up from his place and then we'd leave for the airport. I was leaving a good four hours in advance because Varun had plans for some farewell beers before I left. I could only agree, I stopped outside his house, gave him a missed call and went to buy a pack of smokes.

I didn't even know if I'd get milds there, little did I know smokes were certainly not an issue there and the place had more things for smoking to offer than I was prepared for.

So this was the end of a lot of chapters of my life, school , Neeta (hopefully) and the boye who just kept refusing to grow up.

3

CAB RIDE AND KAVI

Kamraj Airport
Chennai
05:00 p.m.

I'd slept through most of the journey and I needed a smoke the moment I reached Chennai. I bought a pack of milds from a shop right outside the airport which had a poster of a south Indian film star who had buxom aunties on either side. I was trying to figure out how I'd reach Vellore when this man came up to me asked 'veylur'. I said yes. He told me he'd take me in an auto for three grand. I asked him to wait while abusing him in my head. Three hours and three grand for an auto, sorry.

I walked around looking for a place where I could meet others going to VEC, I figured that there would be a lot of other students who would be trying to reach Vellore. I stopped and heard a guy and a girl talking near the smoke shop.

"Hi, are you guys going to Vellore," I asked. "Yes, we are, which year are you. Haven't seen you in college before. Fresher,"the guy asked me half menacingly.

Oh, ragging expected this I was genuinely looking forward too.

"Ok, that makes two, let's go, want to share a cab kiddo".

I agreed though I frowned at being referred to as a kiddo.

"Oye, poetic license, come here, let's go".

The girl who they were referring to as poetic license looked pretty upset and was on the verge of tears. I had to sit next to her as we realized that the guy and the girl who intended on ragging us were knocked out in the cab as they had probably had too much to drink at the Golden Chariot.

"I'm sorry but why were they calling you poetic license", I asked afraid that she might snap. "My name is Kavi and their vague and pathetic sense of humour made them come up with a name like that," she said while breaking into a half smile. I realized she was crying but had the time to notice that she looked very cute when she smiled.

"You from Delhi too," I asked.

She was from Mumbai and was upset partially because she had encountered these two on the flight and the guy had asked her to stand repeatedly during the flight causing her to make a fool of herself.

"The lecherous bastard kept staring at my behind every time I stood and would whisper into that ugly bitch's ears." They were fast asleep which is why she took the liberty of this language.

"One minute, I think I could be of help." Here I was trying to help a girl I'd met for the first time for not more than half an hour by taking on people who were going to rag me to death once I reached college.

"Listen, there's no need for you to do anything. Why do you want to mess round with third years' anyway."

I pulled out my phone and kept it next to my ear. I nudged the sleeping beauty who was sleeping right next to me so that she managed to wake up and witness my fake call.

" Siddhartha Kumar sir, I am fine sir, no issues. What adjustment issues could I possibly have sir, I've not even reached. Still in the cab, I'll reach in an hour or so. Why sir! don't be ridiculous. There was need for you to have sent the car. I'm managing fine except for the fact that there are some students who aren't very supportive of the freshers who join this college, who wait at the airport every year like this to pick up people to torment. No sir, ragging I'm not complaining about but eve-teasing doesn't seem funny to me at all. Names I don't know, Kavi what's the guy's name? I'll just give you a call in a bit and tell you his name sir, he's a third year student. Thank you sir.

The weird multiple piercing woman was wide awake and looked as if someone had molested her.

"Oh, you're awake, good. What is your friend's name." I asked casually as though I intended to put his name on a guest list for a party.

"Sid, I'm sorry but what did we do, listen he was just trying to get to know her and I wasn't even a part of it. He's an idiot, the whole college knows we are best friends. I'll get dragged into this without any fault and why do you want to fuck with three year's of his life. Sorry, we were just trying to have fun." She was on the verge of tears when I decided to play it cool.

"You wake up this Shakti Kapoor friend of your's and tell him I just called a family friend who's a hotshot in the administration. I have exactly ten minutes before I call him again and I'll leave the two of you together in the car while Kavi and I step out for a bit. In ten minutes I'll call so you better have something that can save you're horny asses to say Kavi within ten minutes. Bhaiya, sorry, anna, stop the car. Ten minutes we'll come back".

Kavi and I walked out and I lit a smoke,

"It's a very bad habit you know, it really can kill." Kavi said giving me a dirty look.

"Lying na, I know but what could I possibly do, the first friend I make in my college sulks next to me and complains of weird mongoose like freaks staring at her behind. It was the least I could do." I said as I stepped back a bit to keep the smoke away from her.

"Sid, come here please. We have something to say." Kavi and I walked towards the car.

"Listen Sid, dude I am really sorry for the whole flight thing man. It's just that I saw a pretty fresher and thought I'd try my luck. We are ready to do anything you guys want us to do .We'll pay for the cab, do your laundry for a week. We are even willing to get ragged by you guys, please don't complain. The administration is very strict when it comes to these things."The cool cocky tone had changed to one that Varun was sporting for a week post break up.

"First of all, apologize to Kavi, not me. All I'm saying to you is that I won't complain only if Kavi asks me not to. I know she is pretty and all but serious advice man, the next time you find a girl pretty, please talk to her and buy her coffee instead of making her stand and checking out her behind."

They went on apologizing to Kavi and he went to the extent of calling her sister, idiot I thought to myself. So Kavi was smiling and we were back on the road to Vellore and we, Kavi and I, had the liberty of ragging two people who were senior to us by good two academic years.

Nice one Sid, keep it going, I thought as I high fived myself mentally.

08:00 p.m.
Super mart

Super mart was a multi-utility store we got down at and had our first glimpse of the college. It seemed ok and the market area had a few cigarette shops, an ATM and a few places to eat. The weird seniors had paid up and left us at the store claiming that all the stuff we needed to move into our room was in there. Now this was going to be a serious issue. I had never picked up a dirty boxer off the floor or even attempted folding my bed sheet. All that I'd never factored in when I was making the rather brave decision of moving into a hostel.

"How are we supposed to carry these mattresses to the hostel, to add to it we have all the other shit like buckets and mugs and all of this", whined Kavi as we were moving out of the store. I had decided to play it simple by buying one of those foldable thin cheap mattresses and I figured I didn't need a mug because I didn't buy a bucket anyway.

Why would I want a bucket I wondered?

"Oye, damsel in distress, they wouldn't allow me to come to the girl's hostel and help you out but I think I might have a solution as I looked at the ATM line, Meghna", I screamed.She was the multiple piercing senior who was standing rather gloomily in the ATM line.

I made her leave the line and took her place to withdraw cash and meanwhile had instructed Kavi to tell the woman her room and hostel number so that she could help her by carrying all her stuff there.

"Meghna, make sure you don't drop anything on the way and everything reaches the room safely. Listen, I think Kavi would appreciate it if the bed sheet was laid properly. Then I'm willing to call it quits. Provided her room is spotless when she reaches."

"It will be", she grunted and walked away with the burden.

"Sid, you are awesome", screamed Kavi as she gave me a hug.

Peeeeeeeeeep.What the fuck I thought to myself. I saw a guard who came up to us and said 'Hindi aa,Tamil aa'.

"Hindi aa but why did you whistle." He looked very sad about the job he was doing and looked as if he needed to go home and sleep.

"Yeh hugging kissing not allowed in college, go outside", he said as if it was something that was considered to be understood by everyone since their existence in the womb.

I didn't get it, she hugged me. Outside college. He whistled and threatened to note our names down.

"Yeh lou (pronounced lauu) karne ke liye aaya tum college", he said and walked away disgusted.

Kavi and I stared at each other motionless in silence for a minute. Then we burst out laughing. Loud enough for the whole market to turn around and look at us and loud enough for the guard to start whistling again. We decided we would eat some dinner before we went to hostel and found a dhaba that claimed itself to be a 'punjabi daba'.

The food surprisingly was quite decent and fucking cheap. "So you cleared the entrance to this place too," I asked.

"Well barely managed too but I made it into Computer Science with an extra payment for being a defaulter by not being present for the counseling. I did well in my boards though, got a ninety three percent. I would have done something back home but my parents had heard a lot about this place and though it was required for me to be sent off to this land where the students lech vigorously and the security whistles. Funny na Sid, how the protest here to a simple clean display of affection is done by whistling," as she wiped of some chicken gravy of her lips.

"Funny it is but what is funnier is how I am in the same college as you, through the same method and in an equally, if not tougher branch, with forty percent lesser in my boards. Yes, fifty three Kavi. I know and I can't even pull off the 'I was in ICSE' crap because I wasn't. It was just that I had no options and I wanted to be somewhere away from home when everyone I knew was already joining some college or the other. I'm telling you Neeta, there is nothing more frustrating than sitting at home and watching others plan out their careers systematically while all you do is put on weight and watch reruns of friends."

I pulled out a smoke from the pack I bought in Chennai. I was yet to check the smoke shops if they had milds but I figured I would do it later because Kavi was with me and they seemed rather crowded.

"Who is Neeta", asked Kavi Why do you ask."

"Because you just referred to me as Neeta a while back, who is Neeta. Then again if it's personal, you don't need to tell me." she said smiling.

Anyone else would have got an it's 'personal' but I liked Kavi, she seemed really funny and smart and I thought I could let her know.

"Neeta was this girl I dated back in Delhi for two years before she broke up with me and cut off all channels of communication with me because I responded appropriately to her Dad giving me shit about well, something that's personal, in a nutshell".

Kavi then went about explaining to me how she also had 'mutually ended' a relationship a week back because the guy wanted to well, do a jagran (it's not a girl, it's a big prayer),before she left for college and how she wasn't ready for such a big prayer and how she would never be unless she's forty. I surprisingly , however gay it was, felt the same and couldn't help but agree with the whole theory about how jagrans were meant for somewhat older people and we would do just fine offering regular prayers for a few more years at least.

I dropped Kavi to the gate and ran towards the smoke shop where I'd enquire on milds availability and then head to hostel.

"Bhaiya, paise , bhaiya please". A small boye dressed in oversized clothes came running to me from Super mart.

He explained to me how he was hungry and wanted money, I picked up another pack of milds (Yess!!) and a packet of chips for the kid. I asked him his name.

"My name Mohan sir, I grow up and join this college for needing work bhaiya," he explained while looking nowhere else but the packet of chips. Poor guy must have been really hungry, considering how I could wolf down two of these after a fairly elaborate meal. I gave him a twenty and asked him to buy himself food as I started the walk towards my hostel.

The girls hostel and the boyes hostel were at least placed two kilometers apart. If not anything else, it saved their security guard's breath I figured. The blowing they'd have to do if unleashed in any isolated park or movie theatre or any market back home would make them explode like the stupid nightingale in that Vikram Seth poem which is taught to everyone in their school English readers.

I read the Hostel Rules and Regulations as I entered the hostel.

1. No smoking inside hostel premises.

2. No consumption of alcohol.

3. No noise to be made once it is dark.

4. Misbehavior with warden will merit no warnings and will lead to direct expulsion.

5. No electronic equipments to enter the hostel without the warden's consent.

6. No pets allowed.

Holy fuck, No pets allowed seriously, so I'd have to bid farewell to my iguana before I entered the hostel I thought and laughed loudly as I entered A block hostel. I showed the guard my slip and walked into the warden's office.

"Good evening sir, Siddharth Kumar , room number 544. Here is my hostel receipt and slip. I came to tell you that I have a laptop, cell phone, ipod, digital watch and alarm clock. Do you object to any of them? The rules said ki I had to inform you of all electronic equipment that I possessed."

"One minute", he said as he pulled out a long, fat Bunty and started looking at room numbers.

"Siddharth Kumar, Delhi , keys", he mumbled and he handed me my keys.

I was leaving the room when he said, "don't smoking and drinking in hoshtal, don't make us complain and ruin yuvar career".I wondered if my cheek got me this welcome or everyone was greeted similarly to the hostel by this man.

4

HOSTEL

Room number 544 had a nice feel to it. My name was written on an A4 sized sheet stuck on the wall inside. Karan Gupta it read as the name of my roommate who hadn't showed up still. Sharing a room with someone I hadn't met ever seemed interesting.

There are so many people from different walks of life and talking to a person I'd never met before at popcorn counter or on a street corner excited me so this had to be good I guessed. How bad could it be anyway, even if he was a 'Rocky Chaddha', I'd manage to handle him.

'Rocky Chaddha' was my code phrase for the 'don't mess around with me, you know who my papa is' bracket of guys. In fact I could sustain conversations with them too, being raised in Delhi makes you adept at that. It's just that they tend to get on your nerves beyond a point.

The fact that my room's number added up to thirteen was kind of cool. I realized that I was one of the last guys to get a room allotted and wasn't allowed to select a room and my room mate. The fact that it was air-conditioned and looked pretty good made it pretty obvious that there were people who believed in numerology doing engineering courses.

I got a talk about how the crème of the student society opts for a B.E. as an option and how it creates a breed of thinking rational individuals. I wondered how my uncle would feel about the fact that the rational student crème had superstitious hang-ups.

My uncle was a graduate from the Indian Institute of Technology and he was telling me how this college was the best the country had to offer after the IITs.

I knew people in my class who skipped the farewell and continuation parties of school because they had mock tests in coaching centres which were preparing them to crack the exam which lakhs of kids wrote every year and a hundred odd cleared. Or something like that.

I was clueless as to the real figure.

I hadn't even attempted the test which otherwise is considered mandatory for every student of science in school.

Classes beginning tomorrow, wonder what it's going be like Sid. I noticed students with bags carrying handfuls of textbooks which those oiled-hair farewell-skipping guys used to hide and read in school. They feared the teacher might catch them reading things ten times tougher than what was being taught. I mean, the kind of fears people have isn't funny. Why would you be afraid of studying for something that meant a lot to you and hide it, I mean you're studying guys, not sniffing diluter for god's sake.

I wonder how many of them got into the IITs. They were breathing, eating, living out of textbooks to get into the larger than life group of institutions which provide the country with, well I haven't heard of any greatness achieved by an alumni in any field other than writing books about call centres, struggling marriages and well about themselves.

I lit a smoke and switched on the air conditioning. The weather was kind of muggy but I had heard most of the classes were air conditioned so the weather wouldn't matter much I figured.

"You are Siddharth Kumar," a shortish fair guy had entered the room.

"Yes dude, I am, can I help you".

"Please stop smoking in the room. I am Karan Gupta, your room mate. The warden comes for rounds every night and if he smells smoke in the room, we will get expelled for sure. My father is here, he wants to meet you. He is waiting near the lift."

OK.Hmm.I thought to myself that it could have been worse.

'My name is Karan, my father is so&so Gupta and he will fuck your happiness, if you mess around with me'.

"Sure bro, I have mints on me. Don't worry, your father won't get to know that I smoke", I assured him as I saw him breaking into a half smile.

"Hello beta, I am Karan's father. You're parents didn't come to drop you beta."His father seemed quite nice and had the nice well settled middle aged man's comfortable expression which I feared I would grow up and have one day.

"Well , actually they had to leave early uncle. They had to get back to work. I was with them till the afternoon, I came just an hour back to hostel", I said with my well practiced I was born yesterday expression.

"Accha listen beta, you and Karan have to support each other in your stay here. I heard you are from Delhi. We put up in Meerut. I know you boyes will face adjustment issues but you must support each other in your stay. After all you have come so far away from home, be happy and smile boyes. I must take your leave now. Even I have to report for work tomorrow. Take care boyes."

He said this, shook hands and I moved back so that he could have his final words with his son who seemed quite happy about the good bye as opposed to his dad who seemed to be majorly upset.

"I'm sorry about that, my father is a little protective", Karan said as we entered the room. He told me how his parents were very upset about the fact that he hadn't gotten into IIT, for which he had busted his ass for two years but hadn't managed to clear.

I liked him quite a bit already, which non smoker who had his father standing ten meters away would be cool if someone lit up in his room. I realized he would certainly help a lot with my academics; he seemed like the kinds who would do it. I was fucking tired and very sleepy.

"Don't be stupid man, I thought your dad was saying the right thing. He is going to miss you a lot man, you have stayed with him all your life and now you're leaving. God knows where you are going to be placed after these four years. It's understood that he'll be like this." I poured out whatever little I knew about father-son dynamics to my kind of subdued but nice room mate.

"Oh and yeah, I'll smoke in the toilet from now onwards. Don't worry man. I'll be back in a while , we have to crash early. Classes start tomorrow. I forgot to ask, in which branch are you.".

He was doing an integrated programme which was for five years.

The toilets looked nothing like the ones they show in those movies where the forty year old superstar playing an undergraduate course student shaves and showers in luxury but it wasn't bad on second thought.

It had enough cubicles for a dozen guys to crap and another dozen to shower all at the same time.

This again was another experience I wasn't exactly looking forward too. I finished my smoke and was walking back to the room when my phone rang.

"Hi, Kavi. Ssup, Meghna did all the work. Poor girl, she had to, otherwise she and her friend would have been expelled from the college due to my killer contacts na.

Tomorrow three, sounds good. Outside Supermart is fine.

My roommate is ok, seems ok at least, Bye, good night."

I slept as soon as I lied down and was woken up by Karan in the morning.

"Get up, we are supposed to be in our respective schools in another fifteen minutes. We have the orientation and ice breaking session today.

"Uauhhhahauuhahhuah", I moaned and slept off again. I got up after half an hour and ran for the Electronics Tower. All the students were seated in a biggish auditorium and there was a short balding man speaking. Late on your first day, god bless, I thought to myself as I mustered the courage to open the door and enter.

"Good Morning Sir, I'm sorry, may I enter", I said confidently. There were nearly five hundred people in the auditorium in addition to the pin drop silence that I brought about with my entry into the auditorium. The guy on the podium kept staring at me and I stared back helpless. Perhaps I should have entered silently and found a chair, maybe I should have thought about combing my mane once before leaving the hostel or maybe, just maybe I shouldn't have worn a cheap roadside t-shirt that said 'Fuck This Shit'.

"Well hello young man, I'm glad that you have graced us with your presence. Late on your first day. I'm sure you have a valid reason, oh I think I know. Come here" he repeated the last phrase thrice and louder each time.

I walked up to the podium. "Come take the microphone son, come and take it, he called. I went and stood with the mic in my hand and started talking.

This was an issue with me it was impossible for someone to hand me a mic and expect me not to speak. For the past eight years when handed a mic I spoke non stop till it was snatched away from me.

Absolute gibberish I might be talking, but no chance of stopping No sir, no chance at all.

So this is what happened once the short and kind of bald guy handed me the mic. He obviously had satanic plans of embarrassing me by asking me questions which I either wouldn't be able to answer or questions I wouldn't want to answer.

"Hello everyone, my name is Siddharth Kumar. I am here to become an engineer who specializes in Electronics. Do you know why? How would you possibly know, I don't.

I nearly failed my Board examinations but am here trying to pull off the toughest course from the most prestigious private college in India, after BITS and Manipal of course.

(Ouch, that had to hurt)So I know all of you are wondering why I'm talking right now and not letting sir humiliate me as he planned.

Because I'm not dying to become an engineer, I friends am here to give it a shot. I may walk out midway, I may stay on till the end.

But I'm here for sometime and I'm not going without giving it an honest shot.

So sir, I'm not craving for your degree or placement.

All I want is to be a part of this educational institute till I feel like and learn whatever I'm capable of learning, and doing whatever I'm capable of doing.

For instance, my ability to talk a kid who tops exams will crave once he intends to get prepared for the big bad corporate world where those who can't talk, are screwed to put it simply. I, at times, would want mental ability like the topper who can solve numericals, I can't dream of solving in a jiffy.

It was important for me to join a college for precisely this reason, because it had people and this was the best college that admitted me on the basis of some extra cash and exposed me to a lot of new faces with a lot of new stories to tell, lots of cool things to teach.

This is why I am here, why you are here can be discussed later in the cafeteria or outside while smo. ,ahhuh, eating a toffee .

I'm sorry for being late sir but I'm not sorry for what I said because my, however 70's hindi film like it sounds, mom says never apologize for speaking the truth. I won't sir. Thank you." I said this and walked out of the auditorium and stood outside.

Bullshit you don't want the degree I thought to myself, I wondered why the filmi bastard inside me had to rise to this particular occasion. What would I do in life without a degree and which other college would be as stupid as this to offer me a course based on some extra cash thrown at them.

I wondered as to what possibly the repercussions could be and realized it was ok. They couldn't possibly say that I had broken any rule back there but what was troubling me was who the short bastard was. I didn't know what the V.C. looked like and if it was him, I could even imagine myself behind bars, not jail, those custom made ones in dingy basements of loaded perverts who store minors and exploit them no end. OK, I thought , there's no need to freak out man, it couldn't be him, there were eight other schools having this session going on, why would he pick our's and enter it.

Staring at the walls outside, I started to have an awesome daydream where Neeta and I were, about to jagran when Karan entered and told me we had a test the next day and how he had only revised the course twice and how he was majorly fucked.

Ok beta, what did you just do. Then again I knew myself well enough not to blame myself for what happened. I was worried as to what an ass I had become in front of my whole electronics school.

Beep. Beep.

Kavi messaged saying that her roommate was in the auditorium and had sent her a message saying some Siddharth Kumar had blown the whole auditorium away after taking control of the mic. Her session was over and she was at Nescafe getting some iced tea.

I had seen it on my way in the morning and I told her I'd meet her in five minutes.

She had at least eight guys around her when I reached and I thought I'll get some coffee first. I asked the akka for some coffee and she noticed I reached when she came and hissed "can't you see I need to get rescued."

I spent the first few minutes thinking why I never needed to be rescued like this and the next few minutes thinking how to go about getting her away from these guys who seemed keen on wooing her by venting all their feelings at once. This gang-wooing I was seeing for the first time.

"Hey sweety, you're here. I looked for you everywhere lambie pie. Oh I missed you so much, come give me a kiss" and I went wading through the guys, pecked her, took her by her arm and Kavi and I walked away.

Plonk. Hard hit on the balls.

"Why would you do that", I moaned in agonizing pain that was yet to move up to the stomach.

"Because bastard, you could have pretended to be my boyefriend without pecking me and calling me sweetie pie or whatever, it's so gay."

The pain had moved up. Defend yourself pseudo boyefriend.

"First of all, you attack my genitals then you claim you did because I rescued you but the style in which I did so did not appease you. Fuck you woman. A thank you would make more sense than nut cracking you know."

We went for lunch and she bitched about how her classmates were so fucking weird that one of them, she swore, carried a slate for rough calculations.

INNER VOICE SPEAKS:

Now this is the odd habit of mine which is going to irk you no end, the odd tangential shift I am going to make to discuss things which are of absolutely no relevance and have as much the need to be discussed as did Irfan Pathan's second girlfriend, who if rumours were to believed, didn't exist. Slate is a compound or an element of sorts which is taught to kids who decide to mug twenty five chapters during a course of two years to become successful scientific rational beings of the country, or to sell soap, whatever their star gazing 'baba' advises their respective mothers.

I was amazed by the people Kavi ridiculed with so much passion. She went on about how they carried slates and how they threw her love notes, yes the same ones we threw when we were six , or perhaps younger.

I'm going to take the liberty of making fun of them and deriving humour out of these odd anti-social habits of theirs. For instance their referring to the subjects History and Geography as 'soshaal', or something like that.

But mind you, my doing this does not put them down in anyway, their life was certainly going to be way smoother than mine for all I knew, they would mug their way into a good business school, drive a Merc, marry a young model with assets either bestowed upon her by a God who was rather bored (read lonely) or by the street corner Punju surgeon who had decided the best trade he could indulge in was that of silicon deposits.

He, when in form, would probably refer to himself as a surgeon-shurgeon cum metallurgist-shettalurgist.

I was just happy that Dhaba allowed me to smoke and that I'd finally made a friend who could outtalk me. I was sick of being the one steering the conversation always. She provided me with a chance to sit back and listen for a change. We hung out near Nescafe for a bit but then it was time for her to go back and for me to go to hostel and hopefully start socializing.

"Oyee bastard, call if you get bored at night. I'm not doing much anyway,"Kavi screamed as she walked towards her hostel. I walked in the other direction searching for smokes and a few male friends.

5

KIPPER THE DOG

I entered hostel to find Karan sitting with a textbook. "Oye, are you mad, what are you studying for now, classes haven't even started and I'm sure the first test we will have is at least a month or two away.

"No Sid, I am just going through my course books. I asked my immediate seniors what course books we had to buy for our first semester courses. These are the same you will have to buy you know. We have the same course , all branches do in the first sem", he said with an expression that indicated he didn't like what he was doing either.

"But Karan, let the classes start at least man. Let's meet people today. We don't know anyone who stays in the hostel. Let's meet the guys today." He wasn't inclined so I decided to venture out on my own.

My room was on the top floor of the hostel and I'd seen a lot guys coming in today so I presumed that the occupancy must have got full now.

I saw a guy standing next to the stairs and decided to introduce myself.

"Hi, I'm Siddharth, pretty boring huh". He was trying to look for people to talk too I figured.

"Nitin dude, I swear, this is so fucking boring I'm bordering on knocking on people's doors and asking them to come out of their rooms." He said in a light gujju accent."

He was from Dubai and had gotten in through NRI quota. He said he had alcohol on him which he'd bought from the duty free shop, in addition to a carton of Davidoff Magnums. I told him the alcohol we could save for later in the night and we moved to the floor below us to find people to talk to.

After an hour or so of looking around Nitin and I realized there was no one around who seemed approachable and decided to head to his room. He had speakers and no room mate as yet so he played his music, which was primarily Akbar Sami remixes very loudly. I wasn't exactly very fond of the music but after we had downed three drinks, I liked it a lot more. That was when the issue started, he had been dancing after the second drink but now he was losing balance.

Oh fuck, he is going to puke I thought to myself. I acted fast and took him to the loo where we stood on stone like structures basically meant for washing clothes I figured.

"Sid, I hate this place man. Back in Dubai, all my friends will be out clubbing now man and I'm here in this fucked up place drinking in paper cups afraid of the fact that I'll get caught by the warden. I don't want to be here dude, my girlfriend is back home too.

My parents are fucking conservative man, they could have put me in college back home. There's a BITS there dude, I could have been there but no, they sent me here so that I'd be away from my girlfriend." He was on the verge of puking and I was maintaining a safe distance from him as I lit a smoke.

"Bhai, give me one please", he said and stepped forward. I helped him light his smoke and walked towards the urinal to take a leak.

"Dekh Nitin, we can't do anything about the college now, let more people come, we'll find people and start planning something dude. It won't be so bad, trust me. Dude poker, counter strike, alcohol, cheap pelvic thrusts on Govinda songs, we can do whatever we want man, cheer up. I'm going to my room. Don't you have a roommate."

He was sobering up considerably. I realized the second trip he demanded to the loo alone mustn't have been used to urinate.

"Yes I do have one but he's 'jhalla." He said this with confidence and the expression of surprise and curiosity at this word that he had used went unnoticed.

"Nitin, dude what the fuck is 'jhalla' man. I've never heard any word like that, is it Middle East slang. Speaking of which I have a friend who wanted to know that if..."my voice trailed off as I realized that stud boye had passed out.

I realized my jalla, or whatever it was, was awake when I entered the room.

"I was waiting for you, I wanted to know if I could use you laptop", he said looking hopeful.

"Duh bro, why would you ask, I wont ask when I take notes before exams. I need to sleep now man; I've had a long day. How was your day?"

He explained to me how the Dean of his school had single handedly delivered a lecture and chaired an ice breaking discussion on Kepler's law controversy.

"Oh! Kepler controversy, yeah sure"Kepler Kepler Kepler , the name rang a bell, it was the name of a lame dog based cartoon on some kids channel. No, that was Kepper or something.

"Not bad, did you say something in the session," I asked rather optimistically.

"Are you mad, me, talking in front of so many people. Not a chance,"

If the theory about opposites attracting was true, I would have been drilling extra holes into Karan's bouy to increase options I had to drill him. He was a diametrically opposite person but I really liked him, and Nitin and Kavi. Ok, except for the fuck up with the Dean today, life at college hadn't been very bad. I knew it had to get better with time.

Beep.Beep

A message about how we would get our ID tags and rules for

college. Rules in hostel, rules for college. Rules were promises to me anyway, except with my Karan being the watchful Vodafone pup on my actions, I'd be forced to be obedient at certain times at least.

No entering class in shorts or sleeve-less T shirts, the rest were 'blah, blah, blahaahaha' and I lost interest in them and decided I would play some music.

There were going to be a few classes starting tomorrow, I didn't even have fucking textbooks. All I had were three Buntys my mom forced me to carry.

For those of you who are confused and don't know what I mean, Bunty is a company that makes notebooks and 'copiss'.

So I, during school felt it made more sense to refer to the register as Bunty and perhaps make it feel less inanimate , it would lie abandoned for weeks or months either way so it's the least respect I could show it. I pulled out a nutri bar before I slept and ate it; I had a late lunch with Kavi and skipped dinner because I didn't feel like going to the mess and completing formalities and filling out forms. That could wait till tomorrow.

Punjabi dhaba was catering to the food requirements rather well and even if the mess was brilliant, I just had a weird feeling I wasn't going to like the food there much.

6

ORISSA CAKES

I was up early and decided to shower and get ready for going to the E.T. early today. There was going to be a tour of sorts where they would show us all the classrooms and labs in our block and so that we don't get lost in the monstrosity of a building where we would grind our backsides off starting this afternoon.

I finally got a view of what my classmates were like when I entered the lobby.

Fuck, I said to myself as I saw guys who looked like the first hard on they had was on sighting those inset photographs of female scientists in science textbooks.

The girls, on viewing, offered me an explanation as to why Kavi was being stalked no end. Not that she wasn't very good looking, she definitely was, but unfortunately for her, she was the only one who was and so was going to be in the limelight. I moved around looking for people I could talk to and found a few guys who seemed ok, so I decided to go and start talking to them, when a man came and started screaming.

"Aaeee, get in line. You are college students, why you behave like kinder garten. Get in line and we will start walking," he spat and started moving people and aligning them in files. I started walking towards the end and figured how he expected us not to behave like kids in nursery while attempting to segregate us into two neat files and I had a strange feeling that he wasn't very far from asking us to hold hands and walk.

"Yeow", he screamed at a dangerously thin kid who had walked up to the water cooler. "Did you ask my permission, how you left the line without informing me then", he roared. The poor guy let out a sorry and came stood two places ahead of me.

I pulled out a bottle of water and handed it across to him to which he shot me a terrified look and didn't take it while pointing towards the screaming simon who would need water himself if he maintained the same decibel level any longer.

'Jhalla', I thought to myself, didn't drink water out of fear. A part of me wanted to go get myself a refreshing drink of water from the cooler but I figured should take it easy keeping in mind yesterday's fuck up. I was also being looked at weirdly since I'd come. All these people were probably a witness to my stupid display of emotions and would be apprehensive to talk to me, I guessed.

"My name is S.S. Srinivasan. I will be your Physics lab in charge and today I'm here to show you around all the labs and classrooms where you people will be studying for the next four years".

Then we started the long and boring walk where we were expected to get all excited because he apparently was doing us a favour by taking us into labs where only 2nd year students worked.

"Ooooh, only second years, how lucky are we," I said this guy standing next to me who couldn't manage to spot the sarcasm and agreed with me immediately.

"Dude, you're the guy who fucked around with the Dean's happiness yesterday, right. Sweet shit man, but were you serious about no degree and placement and all that man", said random tall guy in cargos with hair spilling all over his face.

"I'm Rajeev bro, you are Siddharth, if I'm not mistaken right."

"Yep, I was serious about the fact that I'm not dying to become an engineer but a degree always helps bro, so if I have an option between staying and getting a degree or leaving without one, it's kind of obvious what one would pick, right. I didn't see you around when triple S guy was forming lines, you came late".

He looked kind of spaced out and listless but at least he could talk, and he certainly wouldn't fear drinking water in front of a screaming lab assistant, I thought.

"No dude, I was in the loo, went to get a smoke."

Respect escalated as the boye had figured out where one could smoke inside this place. The line no longer existed and people were just floating around looking for god knows what.

"You want to go to the loo Sid," he asked after realizing it was futile to stick to roaming around labs like this.

I pulled out a smoke and lit it in the last western commode cubicle of the loo on that floor while Rajeev pulled out something that read Smoking and pulled out a translucent post-it sized paper from that.

"What's that", I asked like an eight-year old in a zoo.

"Dude, I'm rolling a dooby, don't smoke pot huh. I, uhh, mean that I am smoking weed dude, marijuana, got it yesterday, Do you want to try?,"he said while he pulled out some leaves which he crushed on to the paper and licked it , rolled it and lit it at supersonic speed".

"No Rajeev, thanks, not for me. How does it feel though? Is it like an alcohol high?"

"Sid, Sid, Sid, alcohol is nothing compared to this man. That shit makes you unwell and feel like puking while this, on the other hand, just peaces you out. It makes you value your surroundings more and you feel at one with yourself. Plus, food tastes a lot better after smoking it."

OK, I thought to myself, this guy just said a phrase like 'peaces you out' confidently, this shit must be potent I thought.

We left the loo after he finished the joint and left the block. The circular put up had a list of rooms where our classes were to be held and Rajeev and I looked up to the list to find out that we were classmates and had one class today at four in the evening.

I realized I needed sleep as I was still nursing a minor hangover when I left for the introductory walk or whatever today's event was supposed to be. So I decided to go back to my room and crash considering I had no classes till four in the evening and Kavi had a headache and had decided to stay in the hostel and meet in the evening.

Karan was not in the room when I entered and I considered lighting a smoke but whatever little conscience I had guided me to safety and convinced me how it wasn't required. I mean, the poor guy wasn't asking for much anyway.

'Ab to Aadat si hai mujhko..'

Someone was playing this song so fucking loudly in the corridor that I couldn't sleep. Not that I didn't like Jal, I liked them quite a bit but why would anyone play a song like this at one in the afternoon when people are tired and sweaty and not feeling nice about themselves anyway, not to mention I was trying to sleep for a change. It was more like the kind of song I'd hear a few drinks down or when I was upset. This is where I felt hypocritical for being judgemental about Nitin's taste in music.

It got louder after and a while and was on repeat.

I decided to get off the bunk and go find the bugger playing this song and ask him to turn it down. I left the room and realized the song was being played in the last room of the corridor.

I knocked and a husky voice asked me to come in as I heard the latch being undone from within.

"Hi , dude , the music is kind of loud, don't you think".

The guy was huge, and smelly. When I say huge, I mean huge considering I'm overweight and probably considered huge by quite a few people so this relative huge of mine indicated someone who stood more than six feet tall and must have weighed at least thirty kilos more than me.

"I am sorry, I was just bored so I was playing this song. My name is Shiv, I am from Cuttack. Have you heard of the place, it is in Orissa, come in dude."

He was fucking polite for someone who looked like that and I was bored enough to enter but for the smell. It was putrid, I mean I was on the verge of puking just because of the sheer smell.

"I'm sorry if the room smells bad, come in dude", he said as he pulled out a deo and sprayed it all over the room and on himself.

"Don't know why it smells so bad, I think there's a sewer or something outside".

Sewer, I thought. Pork Chop, I laughed as I realized I didn't know if there was one outside but there was one smelly one inside.

"Cool, I'm Siddharth , from Delhi."

"Oh, you are from Delhi, you must be knowing Ashish. He was in DPS. He is my cousin," he said as I noticed a pack of kings on his mattress.

What was with the assumption that everyone knew each other and how was the fact that some Ashish was his cousin in DPS connected to my introducing myself from Delhi. I mean that school was like a factory in any case. I knew people in the same stream in the same batch who hadn't heard of each other, Let alone knowing each other.

"No, Shiv, don't know him. So, in which branch are you man?"

"I am in Electronics Sid, what about you? Wait, let me guess, you look like you're in Computer Science", he said this after staring at me in silence and trying to gauge by my facial features, what my technical proficiency would be.

"I am in Electronics too, I have class at four today. What makes you say I'm in Computers anyway man?"

It turned out he was just guessing, wow, some life he had , guessing people's branches by staring at them on meeting them for the first time. But it turned out he knew Rajeev well and was going to be classmates with and in turn, with me so my association with Shiv I realized was going to be a long and smelly one.

He didn't smoke pot contrary to what I presumed when he informed me that he was friends with Rajeev. He said they sat in his room at night and Shiv drank while Rajeev rolled one after another till he passed out. He offered me a smoke, which I accepted, I didn't mind kings, and they were like my backup smokes.

He showed me his playlist which comprised of songs I actually liked and we cranked it up as I conveniently forgot how it felt to be in another room trying to sleep with this volume. I must have spent an hour or so with him and then I decided to nap for a bit and leave with Shiv for class later.

Room no. 675
Electronics Tower
04:04 p.m.
My first class in college, I couldn't help but feel excited. It was weird as to how many people were fighting it out and struggling to squeeze in on the first two benches.

Shiv, Rajeev and I were seated comfortably in the second last row and were there because we all knew that the last benchers were the ones who were asked to move up while those on the second last one were the kids who got unlucky because they came late so were seated there. Rajeev, though was, very stoned and was laughing at everything I said, even if it wasn't funny. It was an ego boost either way because I had the ability to demarcate genuine appreciation of humour from you-are-so-fucking-lame, I'm laughing-at-you-laugh but the poor guy actually found me funny.

"Silence, my name is Dr Laxmi and I am your Material Physics professor. Today we will discuss Dual Nature and how we can prove Rayleigh scattering but before that all of you will introduce yourselves turn by turn as it's your first class.Sate your name, hometown and ambition" said the lady, who entered class late and had decided to make up for it by speaking at a speed which was comparable to Justin Gatlin's.

I was just waiting for Rajeev's turn to speak and hoping people didn't come up with very insightful and noble ambitions as I tried to figure out what mine was, at least for this lecture.

"Shiv Pani, Cuttack in Orissa, want to start my own research group that invents useful, I mean good, I mean popular …uh..uhhh… uh…very good discoveries Ma'am", Shiv muttered.

"Rajeev Reddy, Dubai, don't know, who does any way, everyone here wanted to be a film star or cricketer when they were young. That was their ambition then which changed quite evidently so what I'm saying is what guarantee does one have of the fact that what Sid wants to do today or what you want to do today will remain the same, if I were to ask you a week from now or a year from now. As of now though, my ambition would be to settle down in Goa and run a cab service that provides cabs along with local guides for foreigners".

"Siddharth Kumar, Delhi", followed by silence. More silence, followed by Dr Laxmi staring at me as if I'd forgotten to wear my pants.

"You, and you, stand up." She said this while pointing a very stiff finger quite obviously at us, so we stood up immediately.

"Dubai and Delhiaa, you are majors who can vote now, who can roam around with girls but can't decide what you want from your life. There is a difference between what one wants now and what one wanted when they were young. You boye's think it is funny not to be focused now, mark my words, you will regret this attitude of your's in the near future. Styleaaa", she said and turned her back towards us to face the board.

The rest of the class passed smoothly except when Rajeev burst into a fit of maniacal giggles when a kid in the first row asked her 'how one must study to become a topper'.

The idiot didn't realize he was being glared at by the professor and Shiv and I were doing our best to maintain expressions that indicated focus and paid attention to everything being taught.

7

FILAAM THEATRE

A week passed since classes started and nothing remarkable happened except for the fact that Rajeev had started to sleep through most of the classes while Shiv and I tried to cover him and make his sleep go unnoticed in class. The Chemistry teacher had started asking him to leave the class as soon as she entered and I felt the other professors were going to follow soon. Hostel life improved significantly as Nitin, Rajeev, Shiv and I would get together at night and beam out of the sheer fact that we finally found people to hangout with.

Kavi and I would meet in the evening usually and she was happy as some new bombshell had arrived in her class and the stalking circuit had started doing rounds around her now so she was more or less at ease. I had a look at the 'bombshell' and thought she was kind of weird and was glad that Kavi's classmates didn't have my taste in women's looks and had spared Kavi . Poor thing, she was too retarded to be going through emotional distress like this. Issues like the food being too spicy and putting on weight were all that she should have to go through I thought to myself. She was certainly very smart and promised library visits starting in a week where she would attempt to teach me what I failed to understand in class.

Saturday
10:00 a.m.
Administrative Block

I was waiting as I was to meet Kavi , she wanted to leave the campus and explore the rest of Vellore.

"Oye, stud, all dressed up, have a date today", she screamed from distance.

"Yes, with you retard and why would you say I'm dressed up, I ran out of T-shirts, so I was forced to wear a shirt. You on the other hand are allowed to take an hour to get ready and I'm the one who has a date it seems, hypocritical bitch. You are already late by like twenty minutes; let's leave for fuck's sake."

"No, wait, my roommate is coming too, you will like her, and she's from Delhi and is very hot. I'm on the verge of setting you guys up."

She said this probably expecting me to have a humble and shy expression and probably run and hide behind a bush to blush properly.

"Oh, so you have decided to play match maker now, go shoot yourself and call your friend and ask her how long she will take."

We waited for another fifteen minutes when she got a call from her roommate saying that she wasn't up to it and wouldn't come. So we left and tried talking to auto rickshaw pullers to figure out where we could get food and what else one could possibly do.

"Anna, lunch family hotel Darling, I taking hundred rupees," he said and sped away towards wherever we were going.

The hotel as opposed to its rather shady name was O.K. and seemed to be the one of the better places around there. The general murmur one overheard was in Hindi though and I realized most of their clientele was from the college.

Once we were done paying the bill, I asked Kavi if she wanted to watch a movie.

Where though was the question? Auto guy took us to Ad labs which surprisingly existed though it had a Tamil movie playing.

"Anna, Hindi film theatre you know," I asked hopeful that my attempts to communicate with him weren't futile.

"Raghavendra Palace: audio video super quality."

He took us to a place which had to be the shadiest theatre I'd ever seen and I wondered if it made sense to enter with Kavi considering what the stalker clan would be like on encountering her outside the boundaries of the college.

"Kavi, I don't think...Kavi", she had disappeared as I looked around the auto.

"Oyee, over here she screamed from the ticket counter. Hurry idi t, Shahid Kapoor movie." The tickets cost a measly thirty bucks and I almost cried out of sheer happiness when I didn't notice a sign that said No Smoking in the theatre.

Kavi had decided to behave like a three year old since she had realized it was a Shahid Kapoor movie and would mutter under her breath incoherently as she saw the credit sequence where the chocolate hero was barely dressed.

The movie was a mess considering how Mr Kapoor was paired with an actress who looked old enough to be his mother and plump enough to be the…well, to be..to be…uhh…fine then, she was very plump.

"It's boring Sid, can we leave please," Kavi asked when I came back with a bottle of Thums Up for myself.

"Yes, sure, but I thought you liked it a lot. You were watching with rapt attention when I left."

We left the theatre looking for an auto when she told me she missed Karthik as she used to watch all movies with him and was used to well, him being around in theatres as opposes to cynical, sarcastic bastards like me, I wasn't supposed to take offence to that because she hugged me in a patronizing 'it's O.K., you can't help it' kind of way and explained how she like me a lot nonetheless.

Karthik, I presumed was her ex-boyfriend and not a fellow classmate from a summer film appreciation course she had joined. I explained to her she always had the option of turning very religious and showing it and she'd have him back. She wasn't very upset but I cheered her up by singing songs from the movie we'd just seen with a few pelvic thrusts thrown in here and there just in case.

Neeta, die, I thought as I left a spirited Kavi back to her hostel and walked to buy smokes from the shop near Supermart. I didn't miss her much now though.

To: Neeta Mukherjee
Subject: Hi
Hi,

Long time Neeta. I'd mailed you some time back but you seemed very pissed then. I am not expecting you to respond to this but I figure I'd ask you how you are. College is pretty cool huh, I mean considering how this place three thousand kilometers away from everything that I could associate with home nd was comfortable with doesn't seem so bad, college back home must be killer, especially the crowd.

The crowd isn't very bad here though. I have made some pretty cool friends especially this guy called Shiv and this retard of a girl called Kavi, she's the funniest, most outspoken girl I've met. You'd love her, about Shiv, well, he's funny. Not exactly complete wavelength match but he's the only one who doesn't smoke pot among my friends and well has an ability to smell bad just out of a shower also, but I like him, because he is a really nice guy, and he values me as a friend a lot.

I might come home after a month or two, let's meet up then, if you are free. Then again, only if you are comfortable. I was wondering as to how messed up it got towards the end.

I saw the new Shahid Kapoor movie, still like him; don't watch it in that case because it's kind of boring.

I miss you

Sid

There was going to be no reply, of this I was certain. I called up Kavi and spoke to her explaining the whole episode after explaining the whole incident that spurned it off at Neeta's place, about her dad, my dad, the slaps, the mails.

She wanted to meet me in the morning. She was standing outside the entrance from the boy's hostel into the campus. It was 07:30 and I had class in half an hour.

Phat!

She slapped me and followed it up with a hug in pure Bollywood style.

"Once more, dude, listen, once more you mail that bitch and you're dead. I'm serious Sid; you know how pathetic you sound when you talk about that Bong woman. You are funny Sid, and I like you when you remain that way, please don't turn into a pathetic crying wuss please. I'll find you a girl who will make her seem like shit, you trust me. I swear I will."

I said bye to her and left for class only to realize I had a surprise quiz in virtually every class that day, the teacher had dropped a hint to one of those first benchers who ideally should have spread the word but well, he chose to mug all that he could and claimed to have forgotten himself.

I realized I was more fucked than the others because at least the others managed to comprehend a bit in class while I failed to understand a single word that was taught.

The day was so fucked it wasn't funny, we had three quizzes on the same day and I managed to screw all of them up. They carried marks in the final tally according to the teachers. But I knew enough of teacher's and it wasn't beyond them to claim that wearing low waist trousers could contribute towards a student's flunking. I was required to score amazing scores in my internals to have a shot at passing the courses.

I hadn't had a bite since morning and was thinking of calling the guys to dhaba. They had discovered the place on their own too, like every other student of the college but I was the one who insisted on regular visits to the place. Rajeev anyway would either be too stoned or sleepy and wouldn't move an inch so there was no point in calling him I realized. Nitin was in class and said he'd meet me straight in hostel. Shiv who had decided to attack his liver with a vengeance must be in his room with two quarters, so I decided to pack or parcel as it was referred to here, some food and surprise the ever drunk, ever hungry Shiv.

"Shiv, look what daddy got for you?"

He was about to open a full of local rum which he'd been abusing for the past few weeks. I would join him once in a while because drinking with him meant babysitting for hours after the exercise and I wouldn't be sure I could handle that on a regular basis.

"Not daddy. God is what you are. Bastard, I was just about to call you, let's drink".

This is exactly the noise my brain and heart made in unison when I considered sitting with him.

Bzzzzzzz, which in my opinion was good enough for me to say yes and join him. He told me Rajeev had gone in the morning to some place forty kilometers away with some seniors to get weed which would last him another fortnight or so at most.

"What's his issue Shiv, I've asked him like a hundred times, all he does is smile back and roll another, he'll die early for sure. He hasn't attended a single class in weeks now. You at least grace the class with your presence every once in a while".

He responded by laughing and making us our drinks. I decided to go heavy considering I was bored and had nothing better to do anyway. After like a dozen odd drinks, Shiv looked like he could pass out any minute and I considering force puking to make myself feel better. Shiv threw up on himself and wouldn't let me touch him by saying he'd clean himself up the moment he would wake up.

Trring.

"Yes, free, kind of drunked, I mean drunk though. Give me ten minutes, I'll be there."

I was getting up to leave when Shiv jee managed to let out a "dude, are you and Kavi, you know, like are you dating".

"Are you mad, why would you say that, Kavi and I, never, why do you ask though"

"It's just that it's what everyone thinks. Everyone is sure that you guys are a thing man. She is really good looking and a lot of guys try for her, they've come and asked me if I know about the two of you," he was slurring so much I had to focus hard to try and make sense of what he was saying.

"Well Shiv, freak, everyone needs to get a life in that case." A a

8

YASH AND HEART BREAK(NAA!!)

I left the hostel already delayed by about five minutes and with another five to go, walking fast when drunk I didn't appreciate. Kavi was waiting at the campus entrance again and Meghna was next to her.

"Hello ma'am, how are you," I winked at Kavi as I met her.

"This is Meghna, remember, she was supposed to come but she wasn't well that day. I wanted you guys to meet for such a long time", I just hoped that this meeting wasn't going to end up with Kavi's attempts to set me up with this other woman who I thought was cute but mute. I mean she hardly spoke and I'd had enough of dealing with girls who hardly spoke with Neeta. I mean it took weeks to actually get her to start speaking.

Fuck, your thinking about Neeta, not cool I though as I promised myself I'd drink with Shiv everyday till I could be drunk and stop thinking about the bong bitch. Bong bitch, I liked it, I kept repeating in my head till I realized I hadn't spoken for a while, Kavi and Meghna were looking at me intently.

"Yes, Sid, if you have decided to stop staring at bird shit with your mouth open, maybe the three of us could go for dinner," Kavi had made plans for dinner already.

We were walking towards the main gate when Meghna got a call and she said some friend of her's would meet us at Darling.

Great, all I needed was to be spotted with three girls in a college where guys got orgasmic, if they shared a bench with a girl or were slapped by a female professor.

The only saving grace was that we were venturing out around six, this was the time when guys either went to the library, for a smoke or back to hostel. The testosterone count on campus as well as in Darling would be low.

We took an auto and Meghna and Kavi discussed girl stuff while I held my head outside the auto wondering what kind of a name Darling was. I realized there was another place called Baby and concluded that these were obviously brothels turned into family restaurants.

"I don't know why he's like this, he usually talks a lot, Sid, Sid, are you listening," Kavi screamed.

I was a little dazed but I realized Meghna had obviously asked Kavi why I was this silent. Meghna wanting to know why I was silent, I mean I must have been really lost for her to feel I was silent, considering she was the kinds who needed proxy even when she attended the class.

"No, not at all, just a little buzzed, considering someone who drank as much as me and is much bigger was throwing up on himself and discussing weird things like as to whether Kavi and I are dating, my capacity needs to get some respect", I said to Meghna who I had decided to bore by talking non stop to.

"Well, the poor guy has a point, everyone thinks you're dating. I have asked her like a hundred times if you are single," Meghna said and bit her lip furiously.

Hmm, why would she do that I thought.

Perhaps she had a cousin who liked me back in Delhi, maybe she was a mole for Neeta, there you go again, no bong bitch. The three of us realized that Meghna had said something stupid so I tried covering it up by talking endlessly about how Pakistani playback singers are extremely talented and how the opportunities they get in Bollywood are far lesser than what they should.

We reached Darling and I stepped out for a smoke as Meghna and Kavi ordered.

I entered to find some random stud sitting on the table. Yash, it turns out was a second year guy from Delhi, from Neeta's school who had decided to act fresh with two fresher's simultaneously.

He was showing a particular interest in Kavi and Meghna looked a bit upset so I decided to take her for her a walk and cheer her up. While walking I realized not only that she wasn't very bad but like me quite a bit. She asked me about Neeta, Kavi was a definite loudmouth. I managed to discuss Neeta without sounding brash or pathetic.

We entered after fifteen minutes or so and we walked in on this Yash and Kavi hugging.

"Hmm, ok guys, get a room", I joked as we entered.

It turned out the two had been talking a lot for a week now and this was supposed to be a trial date which I observed had been a success. Yash explained how this was a semi-date and I joked about the fact these kind of dates were iota and they needed to get a life.

"Maybe we will, you have a fucking problem gay fuck. The kind of freak shows you hang out with isn't funny Kavi. You think you are funny, stop fucking crying to girls about your heartbreaks and then talk to me. Oh and if you are sad about this little development in your life too, find someone else to cry to, Kavi doesn't have time."

I left and Kavi followed. She explained to me how Yash was a bit possessive and how he was kind of jealous of me.

"He's a very nice guy. It's just that he doesn't like you because he has to hear so much about the two of us," she said.

"Oh, I'm sorry he has to hear it, I'll ensure nothing like that happens again.

Nice guy Kavi, good going. Do me a favour, don't call, or message, please."

INNER VOICE:

Well, Rajeev and Sid seem to get along just fine. Shiva, Nitin and Kavi (till recently) were playing perfect cameos in this blissful yet odd tale of 'growing up' that my protagonist Sid is indulging in. If you feel that Sid is someone who needs to be left alone, this interference of mine is to remind you that Sid will mysteriously disappear (Yes, much like Mohammad Kaif) in a bit to make way for another idiot called Kamal a.k.a. chhotu (a name with which Indian men refer to every four out of five minions working in tea stalls across the country).

The statistics are accurate keeping in mind my research involved examining the tone adopted by the pan spitting, 'abbe ehh' screaming men in exactly five tea stalls. The fifth didn't have kids (I swear!!God promise).

The point I was trying to make in any case was the style of writing that I've adopted might irritate you, but thanks to the brilliant Mr Cyrus Brocha, the concept of having the authors pictorial depiction on the cover page ensures no one shuts it at least!

And well to be blunt, I like it this way.

I always wanted to be able to visualize a J K Rowling version of the Prisoner of Azkaban (which involves the extremely moving, tear jerking and sensitive sequences of a 'to be slaughtered' Hippogriff and a teenage boy throwing up slugs) where the author wrote Ron's version of events.

We move to a time when Yash (yeah, the same one) and Sid are stoner buddies and disillusioned as to what to do next.

A brief recap of events you have missed out on (Well, only because I wanted you to miss out on them, can't really help it, yes, even you, yeah you, the one with the look of disgust directed towards all the under achievers who neither manage to score your marks or oil you hair in the exact way your favourite professor did when he was nine..yeah perv stalker, I know who broke open the lock!!) is provided for your benefit.

- **Siddharth is alive.**

  He is rather insensitive towards the people who claim that they want the polar caps not to melt when they look at his smoke.

  I mean, honestly, when you could have faked cancer, that's the best you could come up with.

  Yash and Sid are friends, which means he's talking to Kavi too.

  Kavi translates to poet.

  Rajeev leaves college (the bloody quitter, leaves his friends mid way through a tough time)

  Rajeev is not me, I'm Sid, I won't answer any questions on this.

  I just realized there won't be anyone questions.

Still, I'm Sid. That's the point.

Sid has discovered pot and is rather delved deep into it for the rest of this book (that's what I'm calling it, laugh all you want)

Read on……

9

PONDY AND POT

I looked at the tree and remained motionless for a while. It had been a week since I had this splitting headache which refused to leave. I had never thought that a headache could torture a person to this extent. I mean, there were graver illnesses that were meant to do things like this. I was just nineteen, why should I go through pain like this. Yash was standing in front of a Tamil movie hoarding screaming endless abuses at the actor. He had decided that all negativity that existed in his life was caused by this state and he spat venom with anything associated with it. Pondicherry was a beautiful place though, we hadn't moved out of our cottages for a good five days. Yash liked the food to come to the room and we were anyways either too stoned or drunk to venture out. We, for some strange reason feared getting mugged; I was equipped with the basic amount of cash that was required to sustain my stay there. He, on the other hand, would carry cash the way our dealer back in Vellore would carry stash. I looked at the tree wondering as to how poetic my thought process had become. Hash, stash, cash, we were abusing no end and the effect was quite evident by now.

It had been months since we had slept sober and had passed out night after night either too drunk or stoned beyond our senses. It was funny as to how Rajeev had left us with only memories of what was a semblance of what our college life was to be. Exams had started today, kids were probably working their asses off trying to pass and do so with flying colors. Yash needed to be calmed down as he screamed at the hoarding while trying to sit on the road and take a swig of vodka.

"Yash, are you mad, keep it away man, cops come here all the time. Let's go back to the room. We need to talk to the cottage guy and shift into one room."Yeah whatever, smile, I've had enough gay jokes. "That way we can afford to extend our stay for a few more days."

He looked at me and smiled, I was used to this smile. I had been getting it for the past few months and I knew this was where he would get down to explaining how fucked we both were and how we needed space to think, like what we had here and not a college where rules were designed to make life so miserable for a student that he'd either end up successful but insensitive and morose or like us. We certainly were products the great institution wouldn't be proud of. Let alone be proud of, there was hardly any hope of our surviving the stay in college without being expelled for violating rules which were designed to castrate the thoughts and happiness of it's students.

"Sid, bhai, lets go to the room. I don't like this place at all. I don't like one bit Sid. Let's go to the beach at night please. We will boom the chillum there. I feel claustrophobic in the room. We have all that we need in the room, why are we here. We don't need this, let's go, and help me please."

I walked over to him and helped him get up and start moving towards the cottage. It had been two hours since we lit the last joint and I had started to sober up. I realized that we hadn't walked very far from the cottage.

Yash had been overdoing the drinking too; he had spent every single minute of the last week with a drink in his hand. He had puked blood and been back with his drink within minutes.

We realized somewhere that what we were doing was extremely messed up but knew at the same time that it was needed. Shiv had called a few days back as to find out about how we were doing. Kavi would have been trying to get through to Yash too but he had smartly done the moment we reached Pondy what I did only a few days back, switched off his phone. I had told my mom that I was going out for a few days, the day I switched off my phone and told her I'd call her in a week. This idiot though hadn't mentioned to a single person where he was.

How we managed to put ourselves in this situation was sad. Why we decided to stay on in Raghavendra late that night was our decision, we could have left at 10, reached within the half an hour, well within the grace period after our hostel entry time was officially over and been sitting happily in college now. It wasn't the reason for this situation but a trigger for sure. Our greased cartridges had gotten us into a mess which had clearly ruined six months of our life, made an entire semester of attending classes and being shouted at by teachers for things like not maintaining notes seem futile.

The committee called off the charges against us but only when we had left, Shiv had called to inform Yash that the charges had been dropped but due to application forms for applying for the final exams being over, we still would be unable to write the exams. What was the point anyway, I thought as I roasted a cigarette, the teachers would have gifted us with internals so beautiful that only ninety plus scores would make us pass the courses.

Fuck it, we needed Auroville beach. We needed to sort out our lives, I thought about Yash for a bit. The poor guy in addition to going through all this with me had been held back from going to the third year because of a fucking printing mistake. Now that would turn anyone crazy, he didn't need this. But nor did I and that's why we were here, walking with two full Vodkas and enough grass to keep us stoned till the morning when the nudist firangs came for a swim.

Either they came everyday at the same time stark naked or we were tripping enough to see them nude. No, a lot of people had told me about these females, Shiv had tried convincing us as to how one of them approached him and asked him to join her for a swim. Shiv swimming with a girl called Karen, I thought about it as I rolled a blunt and stared at Yash. He was a good guy, a nice person though he could be somewhat annoying at times.

"Yash, till when are we here, I have another three grand. I think another four or five days, provided we don't splurge on alcohol."I needed to estimate what my expenses would be in order to survive this long without starving unlike the hero here who was too busy chugging a full Smirnoff, why, I don't know.

It was obvious that we needed this but this was supposed to help, all we seemed to be doing was sitting around screwing our liver and killing brain cells.

"Yash, stop drinking for a bit, listen to me. We have another five days or so here. Let's have fun man. The life we are going to have once we're back in college is going to make us resort to doing this once we are back there too. Let's make this a fucking memorable trip. Let's fucking forget the enquiry, the rotten professors, the machas who chased us around the place, forget it all man. Starting tomorrow, we go on a mission to find happiness.

Super Sid had spoken his bit, worked his magic again. Once in a while I felt the need to be grateful for what I had and feel happy about my life and making others realize how fortunate they were. The last year or so had made this phase come very rarely, very very rarely, as rare as one of those comets that appear periodically after every ninety odd years and passed without anyone noticing only reading it on the first page of the newspapers the next day.

A day's respite from 'Sarkar's' threatening to wage war vehemently against those who had invaded 'their' state is all that it provided to me. But that was an achievement in itself, I wished at times that the comet appear a bit more regularly, hopefully everyday.

"Yash, heard me, let's go for lunch to a good place tomorrow, meet people. Let's find out what the partying scene is. I've heard there are awesome raves hosted by these firangs, easy action is what I see. I won' tell Kavi."

I knew the idiot was high enough to come up with a theory on how Kavi would dump him if she realized, she hated his smoking up anyway, mine too but well I wasn't the boyfriend here, I was just the good friend who she didn't want to see this messed up in her words. How messed up she wanted to see was a question she responded to with a slap.

We walked around for hours and managed to get back to our rooms and sleep.

Meghna had called me a few times, I hadn't answered. She sent me a message saying that she was very hurt about the fact that I'd called Kavi before I left and not called her. It had been two months since our two month old relationship had ended. It was impossible to explain to her that I needed space, it wasn't like I was doing a Neeta, I just wanted to be alone.

Kavi had explained to me over and over again that I needed to be nice to Meghna and how she liked me still.

I saw a lot of movies of late and I had picked up a very annoying habit of relating real life incidents to those witnessed by me on screen. I had a knack for finding situations identical and drawing a lot of thought for perspective formation. I knew it was very stupid but I realized that there were people around me whose actions and thoughts were driven by sheer self-centeredness and vague ghetto morals that they would be better off without. The others just followed what others did or said some oiled their parents and called their parents at the drop of a hat. I mean if the 'leaders' of our country could speak and act according to regional and redundant values imbibed by them from them from other 'Robin Hood leaders', I was definitely not the worst.

At least I had not managed to possess a psyche where I could scheme and perhaps it had helped me be more outspoken.

Inner Voice:

This is where we bid farewell, remember his last words. Not that they are raised again or anything, but well, go ahead, you will feel nice.

10

BYE, FOR NOW

The next portion takes you through the life of Kamal, a resident of Old Delhi.

If you found the Sid's bit's end a little abrupt, well then wait, its not over, Kamal encounters Sid and thus I decided to end both the bits together(a shame I can't incorporate songs here)

We shall end this with ten important points to remember:

- **Only a man needs reassurance, women need men.**
- **I just realized how sexist that sounded.**
- **If you need a pain killer by now, eat it, shut up, continue reading and DON'T WATCH DILLI_6.**
- **The next portion revolves around the charm of the lifestyle of residents of that area.**
- **The Charm! Who am I kidding?**
- **If you are expecting Kamal to meet Sid and alter the course**

of his life and change him for the better. Think again.

- NO, THEY ARE NOT GAY!!
- Honestly they aren't.
- On a more serious note, I realized the value system that people of India claim is unique only to us and it's what sets us apart from other nations is bull!!.
- The discrepancy of values imbibed by individuals across the country is something that needs serious introspection, Kamal to me is what Siddharth needed at that point, and to be absolutely honest, what I needed at a certain point in life.

Now, it's time to take that tangential shift and discuss how futile moderate exercises are for the kind of diet Indian's survive on.

We perhaps are the only ones who survive on combining complex carbohydrates with simple ones and ending up with meals designed to feed a dozen hungry hippos, or an adolescent Indian kid, take your pick.

The need for my depicting Sid, in Kavi's words, as gay shit is perhaps because he was or because my effeminate attributes force me to vent out my feelings on the poor soul who is pretty straight.

Cyrus Brocha once said, "eat till you die, or you will remain weak and unhappy." Well, he didn't, I just made it up.

So as I mentioned earlier and will certainly repeat another seven times in the second half of this book, I am not supposed to be writing.

I'm a teenager who doesn't have college and should be watching TV and gymming, not enclosing my feeling here, for you to ponder over, or play book cricket with.

11

Introduction

Kamal

Inner Voice:

Kamal 'ki kahani' required a lot of time and thinking. Yes, my publishers had to think for ages as to whether something as ridiculous and clichéd should be allowed. Sid is gone for at least a while and in Kamal's words 'return aayega'.Yes, he means that Sid is back later. For now though, it's Kamal, the electrician, the scholar, the rockstar.

Kamal had a rather simple life till he was a seventeen, the usual life a resident of Majnu ka Tila had, the need to describe this is clearly evident but not going to be done elaborately. This is because of the following reasons:

1. I'm running out of time.
2. I don't know much about Majnu ka Tila.
3. Honestly, does anyone???

So here goes, Kamal takes over from here as my siesta beckons, also this is the last (Hopefully) of the idiotic 'Inner Voice' bits. They make for other rather random exercises to torture you and make you lose faith in the concept of the four letter word starting with f, flow.

Kamal's Ishtory

Anuradha'awesome' Reddy

Nayantara Sharma

Shweta Vishwanathan

When a person is brilliant, he usually succeeds is what I believe.

I love it when the comfortable upper middle class of this country tucks itself into it's warm blankets and ensures their 'family pet Bruno' is tucked into a few, only to voice concerns on the number of deaths caused by the cold wave.

Please remain insensitive, we probably would be if we had abundance of wool at our places.

But it's the pseudo-sensitive creeps who amuse me, for instance the politician who claims pollution is an evil that must be fought vigorously, from the window of his diesel automobile.

My name is Kamal, I am here because Siddharth isn't for sometime, and well ten odd blank pages wouldn't exactly seem rather appropriate.

I wont take as much time as Siddharth, maybe because I don't have to, more so as I don't want to.

Read on.

Chapter 1
PANDEY JEE AND KHAMBAS

I needed a break from the class, how could I possibly study in a class where the favourite new hobby was putting ink stains on my shirt.

It turns out, for those who are not from co-educational schools, that teenage boyes, the ones in heat at least, tend to pick on the voluptuous boyes of their class to whistle at them, when not molesting them vigorously.

My dad was a Peon in a college in Delhi University, I used to go and sit near his office, to realize that kids a few years elder to me seemed so different.

The need for me say 'different' is strong, because anyone my age would be smart enough to decipher the simple fact that the Indian youth is certainly not homogenous, which is understandable but this experience of visiting North Campus taught me a great deal.

My cousin brother who was a student in the same college where my father worked told me how there were certain classmates of his who had huge cars to themselves the moment they started, well my cousin's dad was a driver and thus his fascination for cars was understandable, I had my own fascination, something you will realize in a while from now.

When I was about nine years old, there was rather one eventful day in my life, one that was perhaps the most horrifying experience one could go through. It had been three months, eleven days and a few hours since my mother had passed away. I was walking back from school, my school then had been about nine kilometers and a bus could help only half way in this commuting effort of mine.

There he was, I realized as the bus approached the Shakti Nagar stop. My friend Abhimanyu(Pande Jee as he was referred to by others. He was a rather imposing character, with muscles ripping and his t-shirts being a few sizes tighter deliberately.

He must have been around twenty years old, so was the second hand bike he rode.

Cricket is a sport that cuts across all ages, shatters sexual as well as socio-economic barriers, this I had realized at the tender age of nine.

Its amazing how this obvious realization of a nine year old requires a panel of IIM graduates sitting in twenty minute breathers between commercials, I mean matches.

Our prized possession at home was a television which my father valued a great deal.

It was rather big for our room, considering if we were to gauge our requirements and the rooms size respectively, our television would be the size of a matchbox(the one's with either Aim or Joker written mind you, nothing else, and certainly not those huge home lites suitcase matchboxes).

This meant that every cricket match meant the friends would come over and sit watching and drink merrily.

No mother meant my room had turned into a bachelors pad for the men of the locality as they wandered in casually and threw loving abuses at each other while their empty khambas(trust me, you don't want to know) were handed to me as I sat outside trying to figure why these people enjoyeed drinking and watching cricket.

I meant they ended being so drunk they would change last minute to a channel showing a Raveena Tandon and Govinda(a.k.a. God) moving their thighs, which I strangely found rather similar. To add to it a tune that was probably composed in a similar state of intoxication and lyrics which would put emphasis on the repetition of three or four words which translated to navel, belly button, eye lash, belly in that order.

There would be one odd daring wordsmith who would experiment and changc the above order but that was pretty much all I had seen at least.

I was given ten bucks every once in a while and asked to go buy myself a kulfi.

Now this is what I enjoyeed the most about their 'high'ways.

They, let alone them, everyone seemed to forget the pricing of basic essential commodities when 'talli'. That shouldn't be hard to digest, I honestly feel kulfi should be made a part of our staple diet.

Milk, sugar and ethnicity should provide enough reason for this. Considering how the west pretty much swept away all indigenous snacks, perhaps rightly so, Kulfi I feel is one that apart from being indigenous is just orgasmic,

Now, after my kulfi's(notice the stress on the KULFI's, the joye of having underpiced kulfi's is unkown to those who aren't Indian and obese simultaneoulsy).

I would usually take a long walk home and watch the match on a television outside, which would be smaller but at I would get a glimpse of a small, yet amazingly proficient and stunning looking Rahul Dravid.

I think every kid in India has probably been fascinated by the charismatic star who is capable not only of scoring centuries but speaking at the post-match ceremony in English and a baritone that would probably be used only in one of those pseudo-important conferences of big companies discussing marketing strategies.

Not that I had witnessed any of these meetings but they were the theme behind virtually every suiting advertisement that was to hit Indian screens.

Where a father addresses a meeting and sheds a tear drop as he watches his son work hard to become his successor, the hard work mind you is depicted by a smooth creaseless shirt and waistcoat worn by the perfectly sculpted son.

Now well, back home my father despite being in that state would make me sit and ask me what happened in school. I was rather smart at studies, one reason being the fact that I grasped rather well, the other being I didn't/don't have friends.

This exercise of my father's served two purposes for him, one it helped be sure of the fact that I hadn't bunked school to play cricket in the park near Kamal Nagar market.

The other was that it was his was of feeling involved and I continue to encourage him to do so till date.

Well, coming back to certain friend of mine named Abhimanyu 'bastard' Pandey.

Abhimanyu had certainly been to local gyms (referred to as Akhadas).

These great institutions are where the real muscle men are produced, devoid of steroid support that too.

I had managed to make good friends with this much older man.

I refer to him as one keeping in mind no boy could have arms the size of tree trunks, and a chest that would put a bear to shame.

Well he used to pick me up and stop for a smoke as I would treat myself to a kulfi in the meantime.

He would drop me and follow it up with a rather awkward kiss on the cheek.

Kiss me on the cheek, I feel weird even thinking about it, must have been a thick kid, in more ways than one.

Chapter 2
REALITY SHOWS: A COMMENT

Final Chapter -

Before hitting Melodrama.

This is abject socio economic discrimination happening, I deserve as much space as Siddharth, in fact literally speaking I'd need a lot more.

The finer nuances of that bastard's life get discussed in detail and all the random Raveena Tandon jokes are what I get, how the fuck is that fair.

Chapter 3
My Space, Sms'es Grace

I reached school late, this was around a week or so before the pre-board examinations which were a precursor to the scarier and much more intimidating Boards.

I loved it when people on the radio gave advise as to how people should handle themselves around the examinations.

Like watching television, listening to music, and most importantly listening to idiotic unskilled voice artists kill people with their insensitive as well as unimportant tit-bits of vital information for our everyday lives/

Like we needed to know in which non-descript mall the B-grade actor was going to make a fleeting appearance, the sad part is that people actually flocked around these places in anticipation.\

Anyway, in school we were informed that some major Producer wanted to pick up kids from our school and would be interactiong with us for a while.

I honestly didn't give a fuck but how was I to know that this chance encounter would change my life drastically.

The fanfare and celebration began as the nose digging Producer stepped out of his car and flicked his wrist once to make his golden watch shimmer onto hungry looking kid's faces (exhibitionism is perhaps justified in one of those air-kissing, socialite parties, not in a government school jackass).

So there he was, talking about how he knew our school and was very proud of each and every student of our school, I felt all this would have come across as more sincere and believable if he didn't keep texting simultaneously.

The reason why he was here was to announce the launch of Reality Show titled "Indian Newton", behind the stupid pointless name stood an ever stupider crux.

Thirty school passouts from allover the country would be put together in a house where their job would be to solve numericals based in reak kife applications of scientific principles and would have to outsolve each other to continue being on the show.

These thirty people were going to be from a mixed background comprising the classy Convent educated guys, to the kids like me to the Factory products (No, not the one that made the very disturbing version of a yesteryear cult superhit.)

This Factory refers to those schools where the strength of kids per class was so high that it was possible for two people to being in class together for several years and not recognizes each other.

So, anyway, this Mr. Suneja was going to interview the kids from the science batch individually to check if anyone was worth being thrown into his show.

He also announced that the winner of the show would get ample opportunities to continue his education free of cost that perhaps was the only silver lining I saw to this whole exercise.

I waited outside as he started interviewing the kids one by one, most of them ended up coming out looking rather dejected.

I waited for my chance and this is how things unfolded inside the room.

"Kamal, Kamal, Kamal, aaja, sit down", he said pointing his finger at a spot next to him on the sofa.

He asked me the usual where do you stay, what does your father do kind of questions. After this, he informed about how the teachers had informed him how I was the brightest student in class.

"Beta, I see the spark, you have it in you, I see it, I know it", he said as he winked at me playfully (So I wished).

Well, the rest of the conversation involved him explaining how the shooting would span over a week and how we would need to move to a house in some famous studios on Noida.

"Wait, you mean that I am a part of this show", I asked observing how he had already decided what I would need to wear for my entry onto the show.

He told me I was, and hugged me, then a bit more, a bit more, he refused to let go, after a significant amount of carefully executed squeezing, he let go of me.

I told my dad I was going to be on Tv, and took an hour so to tell him that this wasn't the show that encouraged juvenile and predominantly uneducated brats take off on bikes with the zeal to achieve something on this journey, which was either to realize 'who they really were' or show off their cuts and get a break.

The next bit takes you through the several days spent shooting for this particular show.

DAY 1

There are a few people one can never ignore, our director Mr Timmy was certainly one of them.

He entered with a walk that indicated a sense of over-confidence that was unattainable for any other sane person.

His butt was parted as he walked as if someone had shoved up..err..(sorry, er..what I was trying to get across was that he had a funny walk.)

There was a vast difference in the economic profiles of the participants, there were those who had chauffer driven cars waiting outside the set at all moments, there were a few others like me on the other hand.

The way in which this show worked was simple, there would be one person who would prompt the lines from behind the camera, and we introduced ourselves to the 'janta' on the first day.

I was made to mutter something inaudibly which loosely translates to;

I am from a very poor family, but I will try my best to win, if I have your wishes and votes, I could fight my family out of this situation.

I didn't really get why they were airing such a stupid show anyway, they had collected thirty kids who were given scientific puzzles and their solutions daily and a couple of us were asked to fuck up and another would be made to practice an ecstatic expression after being informed that he would be winning the current task.

I hadn't made any friends, as a matter of fact I didn't even care as to whether I won or not, the food was amazing, I was happy.

The menu consisted of a list of dozens of orgasmic culinary delights, I to put it bluntly would rape the food, viciously and repeatedly, much like Sadashiv Amrapurkar (Well, if I remember correctly, he tried at least).

DAY 2

Today was the day I was supposed to be practicing the elated expression; Timmy had come to my room and informed me as to how I was supposed to cry on National television today.

"Why though, may I ask?", which straight guy would want to be seen shedding tears on TV.

"TRP bete, TRP, you won't understand, you do what I ask you to do, stifle a tear first and then say my Father used to drink and beat me up at home everyday, that's when you start howling, follow it up with your voting ID number".

This mofo wanted me to say shit about my Dad who in my opinon was the best one could wish for in the world, I didn't take it well.

Now is when the problem started.

1. The producer Mr. Suneja was in a 'weird' mood.

2. I was oblivious to the concept of retakes and felt what was done once on camera was done in reality shows (if you are taking retakes, why the fuck are you calling it a reality show).

3. Timmy was adamant about me crying and sobbing about my dad.

4. I was not willing to take such shit.

Trrrring: the buzzer rang.

My puzzle was solved,"Sniff, sorry, I have a cold. Vote for me, I miss you dad".

Timmy walked up to me.

Thud, Thish.

"Oyee saale, bastard, who slaps a kid".

Mr. Suneja came and tore Timmy and me apart, interestingly, even I had been trying to get back at him, impulse, does crazy things(my first girlfriend would beg to differ).

"Bete, come with me, I will take you to my room, Pack uppppppp", he screamed and he walked away.

"Cold Drink for you", he handed me a shady coloured drink which tasted all right,

An hour from then, Sunu was examining how much damage Timmy had caused, it was all right till then, then he pecked me on the cheek, multiple times, I was beginning to feel drowsy, almost drunk as I slurred trying to tell him I was fine, and I didn't need help, medical or his salivation.

Next thing I knew, he was unbuttoning me and feeling my chest, I don't remember much except feeling really sleep and gooey that night.

Day 3

I woke up and realized something really messed up had happened the previous night.

I walked for that days shoot; thankfully they edited me of the previous clipping citing me being unwell and thus unavailable for shoot.

Sunu had left though, left a message for me enquiring how I was feeling.

How was I feeling…umm, let's see, violated perhaps, hung over perhaps, freaked out perhaps.

Timmy was being nice to me and also apologized for having slapped me earlier, he cited his being nervous and late shooting schedule to be the reason.

I was checking the menu for lunch already, such complicated feelings and thoughts I was certainly not prepared and as a matter of fact was rather apathetic toward them.

Minutes, Hours and Days passed.

Day 14

I was amazed with the live audience present for the final days shoot.

I was left along with another two contestants who seemed rather nervous,

I had been helped as the 'unwell' bit had been overplayed by the cast with side-profile shots if me lying with a drip being flashed on screen with sad songs from commercial films played on screen from time to time.

(Mind you, Shahrukh and Salman might start bonding over booze, but it is impossible for an unwell , poor kid to manage to enter a reality show and not win.)

That's exactly what happened (Yaay, I know, the emotions don't come naturally).

I won Ten Lakhs worth of cash and a seat in Vellore engineering college, a private institution that was considered to be one of the better colleges around.

The best part was that I was getting a decent stipend apart from the fact that all expenses would be covered.

Wow, I could kiss a certain Mr Suneja now; he for a fact would want more.

Chapter 4
Kamal: In Vellore

Siddharth Kumar, the first friend I made in college drew a very dismal picture of life there.

He was waiting for his roommate and met me only to realize that I was from Delhi, I didn't know where he stayed exactly but I presumed it must have been an up market area.

He was upset about something, so upset that he didn't even care to look around the college once and realize what an awesome place he had come too.

Not that I wasn't upset:

1. The upmarket brats decided to pick on my English.
2. I missed home, everyone does.

3. I'd eaten dal coated vadas on the train and my bladder had invoked the spirit of Virender Sehwag.

But what's the problem that a bit of hard work and vision couldn't solve.

Move on to the movement and realize it's time Sid makes a call, on life.

The Movement
Inner Voice:
Well, endless sessions of absolute futility lead to my not writing for a while, I decided to write only when I realized that it had been three weeks since I spent night after night watching Sitcom repeats and felt stupider by the day.

Writer's block is something I had heard from people who shot me doubtful glances whenever I let it slip I was working on a manuscript.

I'm writing this not because I felt the need to tweak my life here and there, throws in one absurd character and feel like I've achieved something.

I finally managed to come to terms with why I want to write.

By write I refer to this manuscript, or my blog or anything for that matter.

The point is that I have been a rather regular Indian kid for the longest of time and I intend to be one.

One would have to be thick to not realize the inflow of writers from non descript educational profiles throwing light on similar events inspired by their pseudo-rebellious rather insipid lives.

Most of them as a matter of fact do it for a quick buck or the need to highlight their CV's as they need the best 'packezz'.

Mind you, I do not detest those who chase money or lucrative conventional offers, it's just that I wouldn't really care too much about them and as a matter of fact, would dub them phony.

'Bitter Inner Voice' is trying to say that if indeed a certain institute has tormented you enough for you to make a comment on the entire education system and institutions of the country with direct and personal attacks made against yours in particular, what the fuck were you doing there?

This is perhaps the only part of this book that I've written without a break, because it in a weird way, completes me as a person.

I personally want every Indian kid to do well and realize his true potential and excel, mine might be commercial choreography, I'd never know unless I tried, so well, ill shake a leg while Siddharth takes you through what I feel is where my writing will stop for good or might be a step towards distracting me from preaching pelvic thrusts long term.

Now, before this starts sounding like a campaign by one of those dingy institutes that claim they would ensure 'smart and truly attractive carreerrzzz'.

I leave.

Peace.

I looked at the tree and remained motionless for a while. It had been a week since I had this splitting headache which refused to leave. I had never thought that a headache could torture a person to this extent. I mean, there were graver illnesses that were meant to do things like this. I was just nineteen, why should I go through pain like this. Yash was standing in front of a Tamil movie hoarding screaming endless abuses at the actor. He had decided that all negativity that existed in his life was caused by this state and he spat venom with anything associated with it. Pondicherry was a beautiful place though, we hadn't moved out of our cottages for a good five days. Yash liked the food to come to the room and we were anyways either too stoned or drunk to venture out. We, for some strange reason feared getting mugged, I was equipped with the basic amount of cash that was required to sustain my stay there. He on the other hand would carry cash the way our dealer back in Vellore would carry stash. I looked at the tree wondering as to how poetic my thought process had become. Hash, stash, cash, we were abusing no end and the effect was quite evident by now.

It had been months since we had slept sober and had passed out night after night either too drunk or stoned beyond our senses. It was funny as to how Rajeev had left us with only memories of what was a semblance of what our college life was to be. Exams had started today, kids were probably working their asses off trying to pass and do so with flying colors. Yash needed to be calmed down as he screamed at the hoarding while trying to sit on the road and take a swig of vodka.

"Yash, are you mad, keep it away man, cops come here all the time. Let's go back to the room. We need to talk to the cottage guy and shift into one room".Yeah whatever, smile, I've had enough gay jokes. "That way we can afford to extend our stay for a few more days."

He looked at me and smiled, I was used to this smile. I had been getting it for the past few months and I knew this was where he would get down to explaining how fucked we both were and how we needed space to think, like what we had here and not a college where rules were designed to make life so miserable for a student that he'd either end up successful but insensitive and morose or like us. We certainly were products the great institution wouldn't be proud of. Let alone be proud of, there was hardly any hope of our surviving the stay in college without being expelled for violating rules which were designed to castrate the thoughts and happiness of it's students.

"Sid, bhai, lets go to the room. I don't like this place at all. I don't like one bit Sid. Let's go to the beach at night please. We will boom the chillum there. I feel claustrophobic in the room. We have all that we need in the room, why are we here. We don't need this, let's go, and help me please".

I walked over to him and helped him get up and start moving towards the cottage. It had been two hours since we lit the last joint and I had started to sober up. I realized that we hadn't walked very far from the cottage.

Yash had been overdoing the drinking too; he had spent every single minute of the last week with a drink in his hand. He had puked blood and been back with his drink within minutes.

We realized somewhere that what we were doing was extremely messed up but knew at the same time that it was needed. Shiv had called a few days back as to find out about how we were doing. Kavi would have been trying to get through to Yash too but he had smartly done the moment we reached Pondy what I did only a few days back, switched off his phone. I had told my mom that I was going out for a few days the day I switched off my phone and told her I'd call her in a week. This idiot though hadn't mentioned to a single person where he was.

How we managed to put ourselves in this situation was sad. Why we decided to stay on in Raghavendra late that night was our decision, we could have left at 10, reached within the half an hour, well within the grace period after our hostel entry time was officially over and been sitting happily in college now. It wasn't the reason for this situation but a trigger for sure. Our greased cartridges had gotten us into a mess which had clearly ruined six months of our life, made an entire semester of attending classes and being shouted at by teachers for things like not maintaining notes seem futile.

The committee called off the charges against us but only when we had left, Shiv had called to inform Yash that the charges had been dropped but due to application forms for applying for the final exams being over, we still would be unable to write the exams. What was the point anyway, I thought as I roasted a cigarette, the teachers would have gifted us with internals so beautiful that only ninety plus scores would make us pass the courses.

Fuck it, we needed Auroville beach. We needed to sort out our lives, I thought about Yash for a bit. The poor guy in addition to going through all this with me had been held back from going to the third year because of a fucking printing mistake. Now that would turn anyone crazy, he didn't need this. But nor did I and that's why we were here, walking with two full Vodkas and enough grass to keep us stoned till the morning when the nudist firangs came for a swim.

Either they came everyday at the same time stark naked or we were tripping enough to see them nude. No, a lot of people had told me about these females, Shiv had tried convincing us as to how one of them approached him and asked him to join her for a swim. Shiv swimming with a girl called Karen, I thought about it as I rolled a blunt and stared at Yash. He was a good guy, a nice person though he could be somewhat annoying at times.

"Yash, till when are we here, I have another three grand. I think another four or five days, provided we don't splurge on alcohol."I needed to estimate what my expenses would be in order to survive this long without starving unlike the hero here who was too busy chugging a full Smirnoff, why, I don't know.

It was obvious that we needed this but this was supposed to help, all we seemed to be doing was sitting around screwing our liver and killing brain cells.

"Yash, stop drinking for a bit, listen to me. We have another five days or so here. Let's have fun man. The life we are going to have once we're back in college is going to make us resort to doing this once we are back there too. Let's make this a fucking memorable trip. Let's fucking forget the enquiry, the rotten professors, the machas who chased us around the place, forget it all man. Starting tomorrow, we go on a mission to find happiness.

Super Sid had spoken his bit, worked his magic again. Once in a while I felt the need to be grateful for what I had and feel happy about my life and making others realize how fortunate they were. The last year or so had made this phase come very rarely,very very rarely, as rare as one of those comets that appear periodically after every ninety odd years and passed without anyone noticing only reading it on the first page of the newspapers the next day.

A day's respite from 'Sarkar's' threatening to wage war vehemently against those who had invaded 'their' state is all that it provided to me. But that was an achievement in itself, I wished at times that the comet appears a bit more regularly, hopefully everyday.

"Yash, heard me, let's go for lunch to a good place tomorrow, meet people. Let's find out what the partying scene is. I've heard there are awesome raves hosted by these firangs, easy action is what I see. I won't tell Kavi."

I knew the idiot was high enough to come up with a theory on how Kavi would dump him if she realized, she hated his smoking up anyway, mine too but well I wasn't the boyfriend here, I was just the good friend who she didn't want to see this messed up in her words. How messed up she wanted to see was a question she responded to with a slap.

We walked around for hours and managed to get back to our rooms and sleep.

Meghna had called me a few times, I hadn't answered. She sent me a message saying that she was very hurt about the fact that I'd called Kavi before I left and not called her. It had been two months since our two month old relationship had ended. It was impossible to explain to her that I needed space, it wasn't like I was doing a Neeta, I just wanted to be alone.

Kavi had explained to me over and over again that I needed to be nice to Meghna and how she liked me still.

I saw a lot of movies of late and I had picked up a very annoying habit of relating real life incidents to those witnessed by me on screen. I had a knack for finding situations identical and drawing a lot of thought for perspective formation. I knew it was very stupid but I realized that there were people around me whose actions and thoughts were driven by sheer self-centeredness and vague ghetto morals that they would be better off without. The others just followed what others did or said, some oiled their parents and called their parents at the drop of a hat. I mean if the 'leaders' of our country could speak and act according to regional and redundant values imbibed by them from them from other 'Robin Hood leaders', I was definitely not the worst.

At least I had not managed to possess a psyche where I could scheme and perhaps it had helped me be more outspoken.

(The importance of the previus pages in the context of the 'movement' did merit their being repeated, trippy, not.)

No seriously, the only way in which a thought could be made to linger linger in your mind is repetition, try not thinking about something you encounter repeatedly, in the the famous words of my security guard, lassan.

This probably means something grotesque enough for me not to translate.

SPHROOSH!!

That mind you is the noise made by time as we travel like the very gifted Samurai Mr. Hiro Nakamura from H.E.R.O.E.S. .

I needed help I realized, this realization struck me considering how I needed to be attempting to get through this course, but the white flag had been raised subconsciously ages ago and I realized it was about time I came to terms with it.

The idiotic Kamal had said quite a bit, and made sense all the same, I needed to introspect, and do it fast, because change is inevitable, that's something we have heard all our lives.

But do we as individuals possess control over the changes occurring in our lives.

I just managed to convince myself that we did.

Ryan Reynolds is a man I hold in high regard, NO, not because he is married to Scarlette Johannson, but because he was associated with the "Chaos Theory".

I'd discuss that in detail in a while but it was Rajeev's mail that had em thinking.

Here I was, a healthy kid who was smart and yet needed to be guided by someone who chewed up more grass than all the 'Gauu Mata's' of our country put together.

This is what Rajeev had to say;

To Siddharth 'Sid' Kumar

I hope this letter finds you hale and heart... FUCK, theres a reason why only aunties write like this. Let's start over.

Namaste (ironically this is IN the Microsoft Word dictionary!)

Okay, Siddharth (and fyi I AM using your full name just to sound all parent like and life coach-ish.)

Listen, (or read more like), its been a long time since I first saw this fat kid in a 'Fuck This Shit.' t-shirt, who staggered in, half an hour late in our branch orientation and if I remember correctly told our HOD to 'Suck-it' (sorry cant quote you exactly, I was stoned remember), but dude things have changed now, haven't they.

I still remember our first trip to Pondicherry where dirt cheap alcohol and rains meant for a near perfect combination, where for the first time, we looked at the rainbow as something more than just the 'dispersion of light', we were so self absorbed then, I remember thinking that if life did have a purpose, i didn't want any part of it. Those were some of the best days of our lives, and they did really change the people we were. Not necessarily for the better. (Fuck, can I make us sound gayer?)

The point Siddharth is that somewhere down the line, we lost it, not sanity, but as an Akon enthusiast would put it, 'our game', I remember just when i was about to leave, in one of your more 'enlightened' (courtesy marijuana) states, you stated the Siddharth-principle, "If you're not moving backward, you're moving forward." And to this day i believe that makes more sense than anything Swami

Ramdev ever said, (remember the whole 'curing HIV through yoga crap'), but **3 years** down the line, sitting back here in Dubai, I think I can finally see the big loophole in the guiding principle of our lives.

It happened obviously when i had just left Vellore and reached Dubai. Well I was pretty much an outcast in the ultra-competitive Indian rat-race community back home. It's not like it mattered to me though, I wasn't going backwards, so for all i cared they were as insignificant to me as Sania Mirza's marriage to Shoib Malik and all those innumerable court cases being thrown at him. My parents weren't exactly ecstatic, but somehow in your late teens, you dismiss what your parents shave to say as crap anyway, and that we blame on the 'growing up' or the 'archaic ideas of their generation' or even the 'hormones'. See I just had too many things to fall back on, too many excuses, too many alibis add two joints a day to that and you wonder why I just hadn't turned completely into a sadhu.

I obviously had no idea that lying like a log at home with more alcohol than blood inside you was in anyway a BAD thing, and i wont go far enough to say that i was a 'victim of my own identity' (seriously, i want to change the way you think about life but without throwing shit from a 60s Hollywood flick at you). But that's it, that's all I did, I just didn't care any more. So by the age of 18, all I had accomplished in life was being a number in the Dubai census.

I thought that most part of my future was planned out and settled, and that I always had my dad to fall back on for a job, but here's where it gets interesting, my dads company, they rejected me! I mean, he worked there for the best past of the last two decades, but apparently my credentials (which were basically confined to the amount of beer I could chug) were so blotched, that even he couldn't even set me up as a peon.

Well that's when something inside me snapped, hate to break it to you, but remember Dr Laxmi, well that bitch was right! It just didn't make sense anymore to waste away my life like this, (Yeah, just this sentence, no flash of lightning, no ringing temple bells, epiphany's are overrated!) well anyway, I DID manage to get a job, well, you know how they say, that when you get your first job after college you have to start from the bottom, well when you get your first job WITHOUT college you apparently start as a petrol pump attendant!

You know, the surprising bit Siddharth, I don't hate it! I mean yes, I would totally love a Dhirubhai Ambani turn in my life now, but the last time I was anywhere near to having my life planned out was when was 5 I think and I'd go like 'I want to be Suniel Shetty when I grow up.' (WE ALL HAVE SOMETHING TO BE ASHAMED OF!).

I wrote this letter to you Sid, because, I thought, you needed to hear this out. Well its not like you can draw a lot of inspiration from someone who's earning less than a hundred Dirhams a day, but now at least in the immediate future I see myself entering college (and probably finishing it this time and yeah, the foreigner CAB service in Goa is ON!) I mean, I know how it feels to know that engineering isn't your thing, and I'm not saying you should force your ass through Vellore if you don't want to, but just be sure of what you want, don't just drag yourself through life sid, live through it. (Yeah, you get a

LOT of time to think when you're filling fuel tanks)

And lastly I know how this has always been taboo, but Sid, just think of what your mom's going to raise you alone, I don't think she has any crazy future expectations from you, but at least she deserves a son who can fund his own cigarettes!

Remember how we deduced that money does in fact grow on trees, well eventually those trees die.

Think about it.

Rajeev

This is the Final section of my story.

I had always wanted to do bit on characters and how I feel I found a lot of similarities between characters I cooked up momentarily and friends I've possessed for years and will continue to for much longer.

Siddharth started writing a column in the lighter, entertaining and local version of a major daily that apart from his column had a column written by his mentor, Mr. Mayank Austen Soofi.

Apart from these two, the air pecking shopkeeper party hoppers predominated the rest of the paper.

Getting back to what I started out to do, here goes.

For those of you who have encountered this while hitting blogspot online at night, close the book, curse the inflow of mediocrity in fiction writing and sleep well, others stay for a bit, you might like this.

Sid's Parting Statement:

I'm happy now, maybe because I'm doing what I can do, maybe because I like what I can do, honestly coz I'm doing what I like.(Ronan Keating would be very proud of me).

There is NO tear jerking thought I'd leave you on, all Sid is saying is that those of us who have the opportunity to choose, MUST USE IT.

I hope Kamal does well, that kid has serious issues, but he should manage, I've asked Kavi to sort him out, hope the gay fuck gets a girl also.

My articles, a few of them which I found relevant in context to my alter ego Shantanu's,a.k.a Inner Voice's(interesting idiot, thinks I'm the make believe one) attempt at fiction writing.

Do Read.

So Long.

Peace.

Column Virginity Torn Apart.

I, Siddharth , am a regular 19 year old who with a rather irregular academic life as of now.This phase is one which is facilitating a significant amount of time to introspect ...the result of which being this.I always believed there is a need for one to be able channelize their pent up emotions and frustration(hell,yeah.) in a way that is..if not very constructive..atleast not self destructive.

I saw 3 Idiots a while back and honestly thought it was rather nice but lacked a sense of realism.I know..kill me ..but those of you have been to professional colleges especially those associated with technology driven courses,would realize ALL IZZ NOT well.

In fact,im not "HIS" biggest fan considering the rubbish he forced upon us with the senseless 2 states,but it would be fair to say that he managed to highlight the darker sides to college life rather well.

Well,that was his story,i dont have one as of now.What I also don't have is an ability to draw inspiration from others lives and stories,in fact that is something that always irked me.Why would I make a decision in life based on what a completely different individual would have made in the same situation.

Since childhood, Ive been told that there are three kinds of people in the world,those who are smart and learn from others mistakes,those who learn from their own mistakes and then theres me.Well, mistakes can categorized on who faces the consequences of the mistake.

There are mistakes which can affect people other than you and repetiton of these mistakes is unpardonable but what about those which affect only the person himself. Instead of dubbing him a jackass or calling him Harman Baweja behind his back,why can't one try and figure out the persons psyche and what he looks for everytime he falters.

Another question is what the system is!!Blame the system!!A girl died...blame the system...I dropped out of an engineering college..mainly due to pathetic performances which i wasn't used to...why do i have feeling that there are other people in my situation who blame the SYSTEM....except kal tak correspondants,i think no one knows the real meaning of it.

WHY INTERVIEW THE HRD MINISTER IF A NERVOUS KID COMMITS SUICIDE...WHY...how... if lovely jee's tweaking a rule here and there could save a nervous underperforming kids life,then his place is booked in MARVEL COMICS as a new superhero in my opinion....Thats it then, for those of you on facebook,i suggest you join this times of india initiative called aman ki asha...

It's trying to achieve something rather brilliant..anyway..it's way better than being on farmville guys.

A new celina Jaitley movie released this week.For those of you watch it.

Best of luck

Peace

Siddharth

Another interesting one I would want to conclude with is Fraandships, keeping in mind my bud Kamal, and Shiv perhaps who continues his struggle against pot, academics and the bulge simultaneously.

"Fraandships",

I know its kind of cliched now to make fun of the fraandships lot but this isn't doing that.There are extroverts,introverts,people who drool in public and those who are socially autistic.

Mild deviations from these broad catagories and we've pretty much got everyone covered.

Most of the people I can associate with including myself fit into the last of the four(well,not entirely but somewhat there).I read a book a while back by this Brit stand up artiste named Will Smith, it was called "How To be cool".

Well, for starters, if you stop writing books that claim to know the secret to being socially accepted that is the first baby step towards being there.

The rest I'm clueless about and would claim to be always cause it would put me in the same boat as the wannabe "Guru (stretched u, mind you)" Will bhaiya.

India is a densely populated country comprising people from various backgrounds with varying education standards,why pick on those who aren't as fortunate by mocking their language skills.What's worse is the kinds who derive pleasure from mocking people's language skills are one's who at most can be said to have glossy (*read superficial,rather shiny*) English .

Unless one's Amitava Ghosh or a Vikram Seth, what purpose does a language serve, communication right.So there are people who will say fraandships and others who woudln't know better and will do fraandships with them, and they'll be happy.(Its about time we let them be and started feeling the same)

(I have nothing against those who i discuss below,and even if i did,they would never know because a true member of the below dicussed league would never consider himself to be there..small advice,stop picking on people,if picking means so much,try something else, like your nose or a Wren and Martin textbook)

*Instances of shiny/superficial speaking **ishtuds***

1. Excessive use of dude, like, the works...

2. Heavily accented Hindi thrown in out of context.

3. "Seriously bro,I watch only English movies"(I jokingly watch only hindi movies!!Seriously!!)

Life is a race, you have to outrun the others.

Do it guys, by all means, no stopping you, the least you could though would be turn around and give the person behind you a smile. :).

It's not that tough.

Race Away.

Peace.

You know who.